The Cat in Grandfather's House

Carl Henry Grabo

Contents

THE CAT IN GRANDFATHER'S HOUSE

BY

Carl Henry Grabo

PUBLISHER'S NOTE

It is peculiarly fitting in this day of delightful juveniles that an author of many books on the technique of writing should turn his pen to the writing of this child's book.

Carl Grabo, with whose name "The Art of the Short Story" is at once associated, has written this whimsical and imaginative tale of Hortense and the Cat. Antique furniture, literally stuffed with personality, hurries about in the dim moonlight in order to help Hortense through a thrillingly strange campaign against a sinister Cat and a villainous Grater. The book offers rare humor, irresistible alike to grown-ups and children.

It is a book that will stimulate the imagination of the most prosaic child--or at least give it exercise! Wonder, the most fertile awakener of intelligence, and vision are closely akin to imagination, and both are greatly needed in this work-a-day world.

Each reader, a child at heart be he seven or seventy, will bubble with the glee of childhood at all its quaint imaginings. They are so real that they seem to be true.

CHAPTER I

"... going to the big house to live."

Hortense's father put the letter back into its envelope and handed it across the table to her mother.

"I hadn't expected anything of the kind," he said, "but it makes the plan possible provided----"

Hortense knew very well what Papa and Mamma were talking about, for she was ten years old and as smart as most girls and boys of that age. But she went on eating her breakfast and pretending not to hear. Papa and Mamma were going a long way off to Australia, provided Grandmother and Grandfather would care for Hortense in their absence. So Mamma had written, and this was the answer.

"Would you like to stay with Grandfather and Grandmother while Papa and Mamma are away?" her mother asked.

Hortense would like it very much, for she had never been in her grandfather's house. Grandfather and Grandmother had always visited her at Christmas and other times, and she had imagined wonderful stories of the house that she had never seen. All her father would tell of it when she asked him was that it was large and old-fashioned. Once only she had heard him say to her mother, "It would be a strange house for a child."

Strange houses were her delight. In a strange house anything might happen. Always in fairy tales and wonder stories, the houses were deliriously strange.

So when her mother asked her the question, Hortense answered promptly, "Yes, ma'm."

"I'm afraid you'll have no one to play with," Mamma said, "but there will be nice books to read and a large yard to enjoy. Besides, the house itself is very unusual. If you were an imaginative child it might be a little--but then you aren't imaginative."

"Yes, ma'm," said Hortense.

She supposed Mamma was right. If she were really imaginative, no doubt she would have seen a fairy long ago. But though she looked in every likely spot, never had she seen any except once, and that time she wasn't sure.

"My little girl is sensible and not likely to be easily frightened at any unusual or strange--," her father began.

"I shouldn't, Henry," Mamma interrupted swiftly.

"No, perhaps not," Papa agreed.

No more was said, but Hortense knew very well that going to Grandfather's house would be a grand and delightful adventure and that almost anything might happen, provided she were imaginative enough. She reread all her fairy tales by way of preparation, and her dreams grew so exciting that at times she was sorry to wake up in the morning.

Meanwhile, Papa and Mamma were busy packing and putting things away in closets. Finally the day came when Hortense kissed her mamma good-by and cried a little, and Papa took her to the station and, after talking to the conductor, put her on the train.

The conductor said he would take good care that Hortense got off at the right station; then Papa found a seat for her by a window, put her trunk check in her purse and her box of lunch and her handbag beside her, kissed her good-by, and told her to be a brave girl.

He stood outside her window until the train started; then he waved his hand, and Hortense saw him no more. However, she felt sad only for a minute or two, for he was going to Australia and was going to bring her something very interesting, possibly a kangaroo. She had asked for a kangaroo, and Papa had shaken his head doubtfully and said he'd see. But Papa always did that to make the surprise greater.

It was an interesting trip, and Hortense wasn't tired a bit. The conductor came in several times and asked her many questions about her grandfather and her grandmother. He also told her about his own little girl who was just Hortense's age and a wonder at fractions.

When it was time for lunch, the porter brought her a little table upon which she spread the contents of her box, and she had a pleasant luncheon party with an imaginary little boy named Henry. It was all the nicer because she had to eat all Henry's sandwiches and cookies, whereas, if Henry had been a real little boy, he would have eaten them all himself and probably some of hers, too.

After luncheon, the train went more slowly as it climbed into the mountains, and all the rest of the way Hortense looked out of the window. She had never seen big mountains before. Then, about four o'clock in the afternoon, the conductor came and told her to get ready. When the train stopped, he helped her off, called, "All aboard" (though there was nobody to get on), and the train drew away and disappeared.

Hortense was all alone, and there was nobody resembling her grandfather, or her grandfather's old coachman, to meet her. She felt very lonesome until a man with a bright metal plate on his cap, which read **Station Agent**, came to her and asked her name and where she belonged.

"So you're Mr. Douglas' granddaughter," said he, "and are going to the big house to live. Well, well! I guess Uncle Jonah will be along pretty soon."

Hortense went with him and looked up the long street of the little town. The station agent shaded his eyes with his hand.

"I guess that's Uncle Jonah now," said he, and Hortense saw an old-fashioned surrey with a fringed top drawn by two very fat black horses. They were very lazy horses, and it seemed a long time before they drew up at the station and Uncle Jonah climbed painfully out.

Uncle Jonah was very old and black, and his hair was white and kinky.

"Yo's Miss Hortense, isn't yo'?" he asked. "I come fo' to git yo'. I'se kinda' late 'cause Tom an' Jerry, dey jes' sa'ntered along."

The station agent and Uncle Jonah lifted Hortense's steamer trunk into the back seat of the surrey, and with Hortense sitting beside Uncle Jonah, off they went.

"She'd better look out for ghosts up at the big house, hadn't she, Uncle Jonah?" the station agent called after them.

Uncle Jonah grunted.

"Are there ghosts at Grandfather's house?" Hortense asked, feeling a delightful shiver up her back.

"'Cose not," said Uncle Jonah uneasily. "Dat's jes' his foolishness."

"I'd like to see a ghost," said Hortense.

Uncle Jonah stared at her.

"Me, I don' mix up wid no ha'nts," said he. "When I hears 'em rampagin' 'roun' at night, I pulls de kivers up an' shuts mah eyes tight."

"What do they sound like, Uncle Jonah?" Hortense asked breathlessly.

But Uncle Jonah would not answer. Instead he clucked to the horses, and not another word could Hortense get from him for a long time. They drove through the little town and out into the country toward the mountains.

"Is the house right among the mountains?" Hortense asked at last.

"It sho' is," said Uncle Jonah, "De's a mount'in slap in de back yard."

"Goody," said Hortense. "I like mountains."

"Dey's powahful oncomfo'table," grumbled Uncle Jonah.

He stopped the horses on the top of a little hill and pointed with his whip.

"De's de house," he said, "dat big one wid de cupalo."

Hortense looked as directed. Below them, at the foot of a steep mountain, was a tall house with a cupola. It was three stories high, old-fashioned, and had high shuttered windows. The cupola attracted Hortense particularly. She thought she would like to sit high inside and look through the little windows. One could see ever so far and could pretend one were in a lighthouse or on the mast on a ship.

Tom and Jerry walked slowly down the long hill. At its foot was a little house surrounded by a low hedge. A boy of about Hortense's age was playing in the yard. He stopped and stared at Hortense as she passed, and Hortense stared back. Then the boy did a handspring and waved his hand.

"What's that boy's name?" Hortense asked.

Uncle Jonah raised his eyes.

"Good fo' nothin'," muttered Uncle Jonah. "Ef I catches him in my o'cha'd ag'in, I'll lambaste him good."

"He looks like a nice boy," said Hortense.

"Dey ain't no nice boys," said Uncle Jonah. "Dey all needs a lickin'."

Tom and Jerry turned in at a graveled driveway and trotted through a large lawn set with big trees and clumps of shrubbery. They stopped before the big house, and Uncle Jonah and Hortense got down. The wide door opened, and there stood

Grandmother in her white lace cap and black silk dress, as always.

Hortense ran up the steps and kissed her. Grandmother was little, with white hair and bright eyes. They entered the old-fashioned hallway together, and Hortense knew at once that the house would be all that she had hoped.

The hall was dark, and old-fashioned furniture sat along the walls. A spidery staircase with dark wood bannisters rose steeply from one side and wound away out of sight. At the far end of the hall was a great friendly grandfather's clock with a broad round face.

"Tick-tock, tick-tock," said the clock in a deep mellow voice. Hortense thought he said, "Welcome, welcome," and was sure he winked at her.

"I must make him talk to me," thought Hortense. "He seems a very wise old clock. How many interesting things he must know."

A middle-aged woman with a kind face came to meet them.

"Mary, this is my little granddaughter," said Grandmother; and to Hortense, "Mary will take care of you and show you your room. When you have taken your things off, come downstairs and we will have tea."

Hortense followed Mary up the steep, winding stairs to the second floor. Mary opened one of the many doors of the long hallway, and Hortense followed her into a large old-fashioned room with a great four-poster bed. It was a corner room. Through the windows on one side Hortense could look out over the orchard slope that ran down to the brook. Beyond the brook rose a shadowy mountain whose side was so steep that trees could hardly find a foothold among the rocks. On the other side of the room, the windows opened upon the lawn bordered by a hedge. Beyond the hedge was the little house in front of which Hortense had seen the boy, but he was no longer playing in the yard.

A big man carried up Hortense's trunk and placed it in the corner. He had bright blue eyes. Mary introduced him to Hortense.

"This is my husband, Fergus," said she. "We live in the little house beyond the orchard. You must come to see us sometime and have tea. My husband will tell you stories of the Little People."

"The Little People are fairies, aren't they, who live in Ireland?" said Hortense, remembering her fairy tales.

"Not only in Ireland," said Fergus, "but everywhere in woods and mountains.

Do you see that dark place in the rocks halfway up the mountain?"

Hortense looked as directed and thought she saw the place.

"That's the mouth of a cave that goes into the mountain, nobody knows how far," said Fergus. "It is certain that the Little People must live in there."

His eyes twinkled, but his face was quite serious.

"Really?" Hortense asked.

"I've not seen them," said Fergus, "but my eyes are older than yours. I do not doubt that you will see them dancing on moonlight nights."

Meanwhile, Mary had been unpacking the trunk and laying Hortense's things away in the drawers of a great bureau.

"Now we will go down and have tea," said Mary. "Let me brush your hair a bit."

After this was done, they went downstairs again, passed the big clock that winked and said, "Tick-tock, hello," and entered a sunny room where Grandmother sat in her easy chair.

CHAPTER II

"And the darker the room grew, the more it seemed alive."

In Grandmother's room there were tall south windows reaching nearly to the ceiling. It must have been bright with sunshine in midday, but it was nearly evening now and the lower halves of the windows were closed with white shutters, which gave the room a very cosy appearance. In the white marble fireplace a cheerful fire was burning, and above it on the mantel was a large stuffed owl as white as the marble on which he was perched. He seemed quite alive and very wise, his great yellow eyes shining in the firelight. Hortense glanced at him now and then, and always his bright eyes seemed fixed upon her.

"I believe he could talk if he would," thought Hortense. "Sometime when we're alone, I'll ask him if he can't."

"Now, if you'll call your grandfather, we'll have tea," said Grandmother. "He's in his library in the next room."

Hortense ran to do as she was told. The library was walled with books, thousands of them, and near a window Grandfather sat at a big desk, busily writing. He looked up when Hortense entered, and laid down his pen to take her on his knee.

Grandfather had white hair, and bushy white eyebrows over piercing dark eyes. Hortense had always thought him very handsome, particularly when he walked, for he was tall and very straight. She thought he must look like a Sultan or Indian Rajah, such as is told of in the ***Arabian Nights***, for his skin was dark, and when he told her stories of his youth and his wanderings about the earth, she wondered if he weren't really some foreign prince merely pretending to be her grandfather. He had been in many strange places in India, Africa, and the South Seas, and when he chose, he could tell wonderful stories of his adventures.

While Grandfather held her on his lap, Hortense gazed at a strange bronze figure which stood on a stone pedestal beside his desk. It was a bronze image such as Hortense had seen pictured in books--some sort of an idol, she thought. The figure sat cross-legged like a tailor and in one hand held what seemed to be a bronze water lily. Hortense had never seen an image or statue that seemed so calm, as though thinking deep thoughts which it would never trouble to express.

"What a funny little man," said Hortense.

Grandfather looked gravely at the bronze figure.

"That is an image of Buddha, the Indian god," he said. "Perhaps after dinner I'll tell you a story about him."

He lifted Hortense from his knee and, taking her by the hand, went into Grandmother's room.

Mary had brought in the tea wagon, which Hortense thought looked like a dwarf. Indeed, all the furniture seemed curiously alive, as though it could talk if it would. In the corner was a lowboy. With the firelight falling on its polished surface and on the bright brass handles to its drawers, it seemed to make a fat smiling face, as of a good-humored boy.

"What a jolly face," Hortense thought. "He'd be good fun to play with, I'm sure."

She ate her toast and cake while Grandfather and Grandmother talked together in the twilight. And the darker the room grew, the more it seemed alive.

"I believe all these things are talking," said Hortense to herself. "Now, if I could only hear! Perhaps if I had an ear trumpet or something----"

As she was thinking thus, a great tortoise-shell cat walked calmly in, seated himself on the hearth-rug, and stared into the fire. It seemed to Hortense that the firedogs fairly leaped out at him, but the cat only gazed placidly at them.

"He knows they can't get at him," thought Hortense, "and he's saying something to make them mad."

Grandfather and Grandmother were talking in a low tone, and Hortense suddenly found herself listening to them with interest.

"Uncle Jonah says it's a 'ha'nt,'" Grandfather was saying with a smile. "He and Esmerelda are afraid and want me to fix up the rooms over the stable."

"What nonsense!" Grandmother exclaimed sharply.

"But there is something odd about the house, you know," said Grandfather.

"I believe that you think it's a ghost yourself, Keith," said Grandmother, looking keenly at him.

"I've always wanted to see a ghost," admitted Grandfather, "but I've had no luck. Why shouldn't there be ghosts? All simple peoples believe in them."

"Remember Hortense," Grandmother said in a low voice.

"To be sure," Grandfather answered, looking quickly at Hortense.

Hortense heard with all her ears, but her eyes were upon the cat. The cat sat with a smile on his face and one ear cocked. Once he looked at Grandfather and laughed, noiselessly.

"The cat understands every word!" Hortense said to herself with conviction. She began to be a little afraid of the cat, for she felt that everything in the room disliked him. The lowboy no longer smiled but looked rather solemn and foolish. The chairs stood stiffly, as though offended at his presence. The white owl glared fiercely with his yellow eyes, and the firedogs fairly snapped their teeth.

But the cat did not mind. He lay on the hearthrug and grinned at them all. Then he rolled over on his back, waved his paws in the air, and whipped his long tail.

"He's laughing at them!" said Hortense to herself. "And he knows all about the 'ha'nt,' whatever that is!"

Mary came to remove the tea wagon, which Hortense decided was really good at heart but surly and tart of temper because of his deformity. The brass teakettle looked to be good-tempered but unreliable.

"There's something catlike about a teakettle," Hortense reflected. "It likes to sit in a warm place and purr. And it likes any one who will give it what it wants. Its love is cupboard love."

"Dinner isn't until seven," said Grandmother, "so perhaps you'd like to go to the kitchen and see Esmerelda, the cook, Uncle Jonah's wife. If you are nice to her, it will mean cookies and all sorts of good things."

Hortense thought, "If I'm nice to Esmerelda just to get cookies, I'll be no better than the cat and the teakettle; so I hope I can like her for herself." Nevertheless, it would be nice to have cookies, too.

"Isn't this an awfully big house?" said Hortense to Mary as they went down a long dark passage.

"Much too big," said Mary. "I spend my days cleaning rooms that are never used. There's the whole third floor of bedrooms, not one of which has been slept in for years. Then there are the parlors, and many closets full of things that have to be aired, and sunned, and kept from moths."

"May I go with you, Mary, when you clean?" Hortense asked. "I'll help if I can."

"Sure you may," said Mary kindly. "I'll be glad to have you. You'll be company. Some of those dark closets, and the bedrooms with sheeted chairs and things give me the creeps. An old house and old unused rooms are eerie-like. Sometimes I can almost hear whispers, and sighs, and things talking."

"I know," said Hortense. "Everything talks--chairs, and tables, and bureaus, and everything. Only I can never hear just what it is they say. Do you think they move sometimes at night?"

"I'll never look to see," said Mary piously. "At night I stay in my own little house, where everything is quiet and homelike and there are no queer things about."

Hortense shivered delightfully. Perhaps she would see and hear the queer things, and even see the "ha'nt" of which Grandfather had spoken.

The kitchen was a large comfortable place. A bright fire was burning in the range. Shining pans hung on the wall, and Aunt Esmerelda, large, fat, and friendly, with a white handkerchief tied over her head, moved slowly among them.

Aunt Esmerelda put her hands on her hips and looked down at Hortense.

"Yo's the spittin' image of yo' ma, honey," said Aunt Esmerelda. "Does yo' like ginger cookies?"

Hortense doted on ginger cookies.

"De's de jar," said Aunt Esmerelda, pointing to a big crock on the pantry shelf. "Whenevah yo's hongry, jes' yo' he'p yo'se'f."

Hortense sat on a chair in the corner, out of the way, and watched Aunt Esmerelda cook.

"What was the thing you and Uncle Jonah heard?" she asked at last abruptly.

"Wha's dat?" Aunt Esmerelda said, dropping a saucepan with a clatter. "Who tole you 'bout dat?"

"I heard Grandpa talking to Grandma about it," said Hortense.

"It wan't nothin'?" said Esmerelda uneasily. "Don' yo' go 'citin' yo'se'f 'bout dat. Jes' foolishness."

"But if there is a 'ha'nt' in the house, I want to see it," Hortense persisted.

Aunt Esmerelda stared at her with big eyes.

"Who all said anythin' 'bout dis yere ha'nt? I ain't never heard of no ha'nt."

"When you hear it again, please wake me up if I'm asleep," said Hortense.

"Heavens, I don' get outa' mah bed w'en I hears nothin'," said Aunt Esmerelda. "Not by no means. E'n if yo' hears anythin', jes' yo' shut yo' eahs and pull the kivers ovah yo' head. Den dey don' git yo'."

But Hortense felt quite brave by the bright kitchen fire. She sat very quietly and watched Aunt Esmerelda at work. The kitchen was filled with bright friendly things--shining pans and spoons, a squat, fat milk jug with a smiling face, a rolling pin that looked very stupid, an egg beater that surely must get as dizzy as a whirling dervish turning round and round very fast--probably quite a scatterbrain, Hortense thought.

"What is that, Aunt Esmerelda?" Hortense asked, pointing to a bright rounded utensil hanging above the kitchen table.

Aunt Esmerelda looked.

"Dat's a grater, chile. I grates cheese an' potatoes an' cabbage an' things wid dat."

She took down the grater.

"On dis side it grates things small and on dis side big."

She hung it in its place again.

"It looks wicked to me," said Hortense. "I shouldn't like to meet it wandering around the house at night."

"Laws, chile, how yo' talks," Aunt Esmerelda exclaimed startled. "Yo' gives me de fidgets. Wheh yo' git ideas like dat?"

"Things look that way," said Hortense. "Some look friendly and some unfriendly. There's the cat and the teakettle. They aren't friendly. They say all sorts of sly things. Sometime I'm going to hear what they are. The grater would run after you and scrape you on his sharp sides if he could."

Aunt Esmerelda shook her head uneasily. From time to time she stared at Hortense.

"Yo's a curyus chile," she muttered. "I don' know what yo' ma means a-bringin' yo' up disaway, scaihin' po' ole Aunt Esmerelda. Lan's sakes, if I ain't done forgit de pertatahs! An' dey's all in de stoh'room!"

"Where's that?" Hortense asked much interested.

"In de basement," said Aunt Esmerelda, "an' it's powahful dark down deh."

"I'll go with you," said Hortense eagerly. "I'd like to see it."

Aunt Esmerelda lighted a candle and, taking a large pan, opened the door leading to the basement.

It was a large basement, and the candle was not sufficient to light its more remote corners. They passed a huge dark furnace with its arms stretching out on all sides like a spider's legs. In front of it was a coal bin, large and black.

Aunt Esmerelda opened the door of the storeroom. Within were barrels and boxes, and hanging shelves laden with row upon row of preserves in jars and regiments of jelly glasses, each with its paper top and its white label.

Aunt Esmerelda filled her pan with potatoes from the barrel and led the way from the storeroom. Closing the door, she led the way back upstairs.

A sudden noise of something falling and of little scurrying feet led her to stop abruptly. Hortense drew close to her. Aunt Esmerelda was shaking, and by the light of the candle Hortense could see the whites of her eyes gleaming as she looked all about her.

They started again for the cellar stairs. When they had reached the furnace, a sudden gust of wind blew out the candle. In a far corner of the cellar something rattled.

Aunt Esmerelda started to run, and Hortense ran after her. A faint light from the kitchen shone on the head of the cellar stairs. Aunt Esmerelda hurried up the stairs, panting, with Hortense at her heels. At the top Aunt Esmerelda slammed and bolted the door; then she sank into a chair and mopped her perspiring face.

"Do you think it was the 'ha'nt'?" Hortense asked much excited.

"Don' speak to me 'bout no ha'nt!" exclaimed Aunt Esmerelda angrily. "Yo' sho' scaihs me. Run along and git ready fo' dinnah."

Though Hortense lingered, Aunt Esmerelda would not say another word, and finally Hortense went to change her dress.

CHAPTER III

"They could hear the soft pat-pat of padded feet in the hall."

Dinner was served in the large dining room. Friendly clusters of candles stood on the round mahogany table and made little pools of light on its bright surface. Mary waited on them.

"I wonder what's the matter with Aunt Esmerelda to-night," said Grandpa after the soup. "These potatoes aren't done, and the roast is burned."

"I think she was frightened at something in the cellar," said Hortense.

"What's that?" Grandpa questioned, and Hortense told him of the noise and the candle going out.

"A rat probably," said Grandpa. "Weren't you frightened?"

"A little," Hortense replied truthfully, "but I think it was because Aunt Esmerelda was so afraid."

Grandpa looked at her, smiling under his bushy eyebrows.

"Would you go down to the storeroom and get me an apple if I gave you something nice for your own?" he asked.

"Don't, Keith," said Grandma sharply. "You'll frighten the child."

"I don't want her to be afraid in the dark," said Grandpa. "This is a big house and much of it is dark."

Hortense was silent, thinking.

"I'll go," she said.

"Good," said Grandpa. "Bring me a plateful of northern spies."

Hortense arose from the table and walked to the door. As she went out, she heard Grandmother say, "You'll frighten the child----" The rest she didn't hear.

In the kitchen Hortense found Aunt Esmerelda seated in her chair, gazing gloomily at the kitchen range.

"May I have a candle, Aunt Esmerelda?" Hortense asked.

"What fo' yo' wants a candle?" Aunt Esmerelda demanded.

"I'm going to the storeroom to get Grandpa some apples," said Hortense.

Aunt Esmerelda stared at her without speaking for some moments.

"All by yo'se'f?" she demanded at last.

"All by myself," said Hortense.

Aunt Esmerelda shook her head and muttered, but rising, found a candle and lighted it.

"Ef yo' say yo' prayahs, mebbe nothin'll git yo'," she said ominously.

It was black as a hat in the basement, and little shivers ran up and down Hortense's spine, but she ran quickly to the storeroom and filled her plate with apples from the big barrel.

Starting back she heard a noise and stopped, her heart pounding and little pin pricks crinkling her scalp; then she hurried to the stairs, almost running. But she did not run up the stairs, for she didn't wish to have Aunt Esmerelda think her afraid.

She was a glad little girl, nevertheless, when she was safe again in the light kitchen.

"Yo' didn' see nothin'?" demanded Aunt Esmerelda.

"I didn't see anything," said Hortense. "I heard something, but it was probably only a rat." She spoke bravely, quite like Grandfather.

"'Twan't no rat," muttered Aunt Esmerelda gloomily, shaking her head. "It's a ha'nt or a ghos'. Dey's ha'nts and ghos's all 'roun dis place."

Hortense began to feel quite brave after she had arrived safely in the cheerful dining room. Grandfather looked at her, shrewdly smiling.

"Did you see or hear anything?" he asked.

"I heard--a noise," replied Hortense.

"And were you afraid?" he asked again.

Hortense looked into his bright, kind eyes.

"A little," she confessed.

Grandfather took her on his knee.

"It isn't being afraid that matters," he said. "It's doing what you set out to do whether afraid or not That's what it is to be brave."

"Really?" Hortense asked.

"Yes, really," assured Grandfather. "It is not brave to be without fear, but to overcome it. Now we'll go into the library, and I'll tell you the promised story and give you something--but what it is, I'll not reveal until later."

Grandmother returned to her chair and her knitting, with the white owl and the cat for company, and Grandfather and Hortense found a comfortable seat in Grandfather's big chair. There was a cheerful fire on the hearth, and Grandfather's study lamp cast a bright light upon his desk--but the bronze Buddha remained in a shadow, and the rows of books along the walls were scarcely visible.

"When I was a young lad in Scotland," said Grandfather when Hortense was seated on his knee with her head upon his shoulder, "I had a close friend of my own age whose name was Dugald--Dugald Stewart. We grew up together, and when we became young men, we set off together to see the world and to make our fortunes.

"We visited many strange and wonderful places and had many adventures, some of which I shall tell you about, perhaps. Our fortunes were up and down, usually down. We sought for pearls in the Indian Ocean and the South Seas, and for gold in Australia. We traded with the natives here, there, and everywhere, but our fortunes were still to be made, and it seemed we might spend our lives without being much better off than we were then.

"At last Dugald and I parted company. I was to go on a trading journey into the interior of Borneo, which, as you know, is a very large island in the East Indies. Dugald set out upon a wild expedition into Burma. We had heard a story of a rare and valuable jewel said to be in a remote and little-known part of the interior. I had tried to dissuade him from so dangerous and uncertain an attempt, but he was brave and even reckless. Besides, my own adventure was dangerous also.

"Before we parted, Dugald gave me a little charm which he always wore and in which he had great faith. It was supposed to bring luck and to shield from danger. Perhaps it did, for I was very lucky thereafter and had many wonderful escapes from death. It was not so with Dugald. I never saw him again, and I wish now that he had kept the charm. Perhaps it would have protected him."

Grandfather paused and glanced at the bronze figure of Buddha beyond the circle of the lamplight.

"This image was his last gift to me, brought by his trusted servant with the message that in it lay fortune and that I should always keep it by me--and I have always done so."

"Did he find the valuable jewel?" Hortense asked breathlessly.

"That I never knew," said Grandfather. "The servant told me a wild story of his master's finding it, but when my friend died suddenly, the servant could find no trace of it. I think he was honest, too.

"But the jewel isn't the point of my story--rather, the charm."

Grandfather opened a drawer of his desk and drew forth a tiny box of sweet smelling wood--sandalwood, Grandfather called it. He bade Hortense lift the cover. Inside the box lay a tiny ivory monkey attached to a tarnished silver chain.

"It can be worn around the neck," said Grandfather, drawing it forth. Placing the chain about Hortense's neck, he fastened the ends in a secure little clasp.

"Now you'll have good luck and nothing can harm you," he said smiling at her.

"Is it mine?" Hortense asked.

"You may wear it while you are here," said Grandfather, "and sometime it will be yours for keeps."

"And I won't be afraid of noises or anything," said Hortense.

"Not a thing can hurt you," said Grandfather. "But you must take good care not to lose it. You had better wear it under your dress, perhaps, and never take it off. Now, it is long past bedtime."

Hortense thanked her Grandfather and went into the next room to bid her Grandmother good night. Lowboy, fat and smiling, grinned at her. The cat on the hearthrug turned his head and regarded her with a long stare from his yellow eyes. Hortense felt uncomfortable but stared back, and at last the cat turned away and pretended to wash himself. Now and then he stole a glance at her out of the corner of his eye.

"He doesn't like me any more than I like him," thought Hortense as she kissed her Grandmother good night.

"Your candle is on the table in the hall, dear," said Grandmother. "Would you like Mary to put you to bed?"

But Hortense felt very brave after her exploit in the storeroom; besides which, her monkey charm gave her a sense of security. She lighted her candle and set off up the dark winding stairs all alone.

When she reached the second floor, she stopped and looked up the stairs leading to the third floor. She could see only a little way and she longed to know what it was like up there, but she felt a little timid at the thought of all those empty rooms filled with cold, silent furniture. What was it Grandfather had said? Always to face the thing one feared.

Hortense marched bravely up the stairs to the hall above. It was like that on the second floor. Hortense opened one of the many closed doors. The light from her candle fell upon chairs and dressers sheeted like ghosts, cold and silent. Hortense shut the door quickly and walked past all the others without opening them.

At the end of the hall was a door somewhat smaller than the others. It seemed mysterious, and after hesitating for a moment, Hortense turned the knob slowly.

A flight of steps rose steeply from the threshold. Hortense peered up. Above, it was faintly light These must be the attic stairs, Hortense thought, and the attic was not completely dark because the cupola lighted it faintly. When the moon was bright, it would be possible to see quite plainly. Perhaps on such a night or, better, in the daytime, Hortense would explore the attic, but she felt she had done enough for one night and closed the door gently.

As she turned to walk back down the hall, she stopped suddenly. Far away in the dark gleamed two yellow spots. Chills ran up her back, and then she told herself, "It's the cat."

Slowly she walked towards the bright spots which never moved as she neared them. Then the rays from her candle fell upon the cat crouched in the middle of the hall.

"What are you doing, spying on me like this!" said Hortense severely.

The cat said not a word. He merely stared at her with his bright yellow eyes for a moment; then he yawned, rose slowly and stretched himself, and turning, walked with dignity down the stairs. Hortense followed, but not once did the cat look back at her.

On the second floor Hortense stopped and watched the cat. When he was lost to sight in the hall below, she went to her room and carefully closed the door behind her.

She placed her candle on a stand beside the bed and proceeded to look around.

The room seemed much bigger now than in the afternoon. The ceiling seemed lost in shadow far above, and the corners were all dark. There were three stiff chairs, a table, a dresser, and a highboy.

The highboy was tall and slim. The light from the candle made him seem very melancholy and sad, ridiculously so, Hortense thought.

"You are funny looking," said Hortense aloud.

The highboy, she thought, regarded her reproachfully.

"Why don't you speak?" said Hortense, "instead of looking so woebegone."

"You'll only make fun of me," said Highboy in a tearful voice.

"No, I won't," Hortense replied, "not if you'll try to look and talk a bit cheerful."

"That's easy to say," said Highboy, "but you don't have to stay in this room day and night with nobody to talk to. It gets on my nerves."

"I'll talk to you," said Hortense, "but you should cultivate a cheerful disposition. I like bright people."

"Then you'd better talk with my brother, Lowboy," said Highboy tartly. "He's always cheery. Nothing depresses me so much as people who are always cheerful. Tiresome, I say."

"You could learn much from your brother," said Hortense severely. "Why don't you go down and see him now? I'm sure it would do you good."

Highboy shivered.

"It's so cold and dark in the hall," he said. "I almost never dare go except on bright warm nights in summer. Of course I daren't go in the daytime."

"No, I suppose not," said Hortense. "However, I'll go with you, you are afraid. Grandmother has gone to bed, I think, and there will be a little fire left on the hearth."

Highboy brightened a little.

"Do you think we dare?" he said, "Suppose we should meet the cat."

"I'm not afraid of the cat," Hortense declared.

"And then there's the other one," said Highboy. "He's worse still. He's round, and bright, and hard, with sharp points all over--a terrible fellow."

"Is he the 'ha'nt,' as Aunt Esmerelda calls it?" Hortense asked.

Highboy knew nothing about that. He was only sure that the cat, Jeremiah, and his prickly companion were up to all manner of tricks and were best let alone.

Hortense, on second thought, did not wholly relish the idea of going downstairs with Highboy, but she had made the offer and so she said, "Come on, we'll go now, for I mustn't stay up too late."

Highboy stepped out of his wooden house. He looked so funny in his knee trousers and broad white collar with its big bow tie, exactly like a great overgrown boy, that Hortense laughed out loud.

"If you laugh at me, I won't go," said Highboy in a mournful voice.

"I beg your pardon," said Hortense. "It was rude of me. But you should wear long trousers you know! You are too big to wear such things as these."

"I know it," said Highboy, "but I can't change. I haven't any others. Besides, I've always worn them and I'd not feel the same in anything different. One gets awfully attached to old clothes, don't you think?"

"Boys do, I've observed," said Hortense. "Come on."

She took Highboy by the hand, and they walked cautiously down the hall. At the top of the stairs Highboy paused and leaned over the bannisters. Somebody was walking to and fro in the hall beneath with soft regular footfalls like the ticking of a clock.

"It's only Grandfather's Clock," said Highboy in a relieved whisper. "He always walks that way at night."

Highboy and Hortense descended the stairs into the hall. Grandfather's Clock was walking up and down with regular footfalls, tick-tock, tick-tock. He smiled benevolently at them as they passed but did not pause in his walk or speak to them.

"A dull life," said Highboy. "Duller than mine. You see, he has nothing to be afraid of. To be afraid of something gives you a thrill, you know. But everybody's afraid of time, and Grandfather's Clock has all the time there is."

When Hortense and Highboy entered, only the embers of the fire were left on the hearth in Grandmother's room. White Owl was wide-awake with staring eyes, but the Firedogs were evidently napping and Lowboy was sound asleep.

"Hello," said Highboy, and at once Lowboy's eyes opened wide and both the Firedogs growled.

"Come out and talk," said Highboy.

Lowboy obeyed at once. He was short and fat--not half so tall as his brother, but twice as big around--and he was dressed exactly like Highboy except that his necktie was red whereas Highboy's tie was green.

"I knew she'd bring you," said Lowboy, pointing to Hortense. "I could see she was friendly."

"She may only be a meddlesome child," said White Owl. "It never does to judge from first impressions."

"I could see that the cat didn't like her," said one of the firedogs, shaking himself and coming out upon the hearthrug, "and anybody that the cat dislikes is a friend of mine."

"Just so," said the other firedog.

They were just alike.

"I know I can never tell you apart," said Hortense. "What are your names?"

"Mine's Coal and his is Ember," said the first firedog, "and you can always tell us in this way: If you call me Ember and I don't answer, then you'll know I'm Coal. It's very easy! But if you'll look close, you'll see that my tail curls a little tighter than his, and I'm generally thought to be handsomer."

"You're not," said Ember. "Say that again and I'll fight you."

"Oh, please don't fight!" cried Hortense. "However can you chase the cat if you do?"

"That's the first sensible remark any one has made," said White Owl.

"I apologize," said Coal to Ember. "Let's not fight unless there's nothing else to do."

"Fighting is an occupation for those who don't think," said White Owl.

Lowboy nudged his brother.

"Talks just like a copy book, doesn't he?" said Lowboy.

"He has to keep up his reputation," said Highboy.

"Ssh," said White Owl, "I hear the cat."

Everybody became as still as a mouse. Coal and Ember crouched, ready to spring, and Highboy and Lowboy, rather frightened, took hold of hands and pressed against the wall. They could hear the soft pat-pat of padded feet in the hall.

Two yellow eyes shone in the doorway, and the Cat entered. He stood in the middle of the room with his tail waving to and fro and looked suspiciously from side to side.

Both Firedogs growled; the Cat spit; White Owl cried, "Who-oo-o," and flew down from his perch. In a twinkling Hortense was running down the hall, hand in hand with Highboy and Lowboy, behind Coal and Ember.

Up the stairs ran the Cat with the Firedogs after him, up the stairs to the third floor and through the door to the attic.

"I'm sure I shut that door," said Hortense. "Who could have opened it?"

She had no time to think further. Up and up she went to the attic and there stopped, panting. The Firedogs were running round and round, growling. White Owl turned his great yellow eyes in all directions.

"He isn't here," said Owl. "I can see in every corner, and he isn't here. But where could he have gone?"

Nobody had an answer to make, and every one felt that there was something mysterious in the Cat's sudden disappearance.

"I think I'd better go back," said Highboy nervously. "It's time I was asleep. Suppose we should be found way up here!"

By common consent they all moved downstairs together, going very softly. Hortense paused at Grandmother's door. She was speaking.

"I'm sure I heard something," said Grandmother.

"It was only the wind," Grandfather's voice replied.

Hortense and Highboy crept quietly to their room while the others disappeared below.

"It's good to be back safe," Highboy whispered, "but I'm so nervous I know I shan't sleep."

Hortense, however, undressed quickly and climbed into bed. Soon she was fast asleep, and the next thing she knew the sun was shining into her windows.

"It must have been a dream," said Hortense to herself, remembering all that had happened the evening before.

"Was it a dream, Highboy?" she said suddenly, looking at him.

"You may have dreamed," said Highboy irritably, "but I was so nervous I didn't sleep a wink."

Saying no more, Hortense dressed rapidly and went down to breakfast.

CHAPTER IV

"Highboy, and Lowboy, and Owl, and the Firedogs come out at night."

When Grandmother asked at breakfast if she had slept well, Hortense replied truthfully that she had.

"I don't know what got into Jeremiah last night," said Grandmother. "I heard something myself, and Esmerelda declares he ran about the house like one possessed. This morning we heard him in the attic."

Hortense, eating her egg and toast, thought she might tell Grandmother of last night's surprising events, but of course she wouldn't be believed. So on second thought she said nothing.

Slipping away to the kitchen when breakfast was over, she found Jeremiah begging for his breakfast and Aunt Esmerelda regarding him with hands on hips, shaking her head.

"Yo' sho' is possessed," said Aunt Esmerelda. "Such carrying on I never heard. I spec's de evil one was after yo', an' I hopes he catches yo' and takes yo' away wid him."

Jeremiah winked his yellow eyes sleepily in reply, but at the sight of Hortense he lashed his tail and turned away. Aunt Esmerelda, grumbling, gave him a saucer of milk.

"Yo' keep away from dat animal," said Aunt Esmerelda to Hortense. "No one knows de wickedness of his heart."

Hortense waited in the kitchen until Mary was free to begin her morning's task of dusting and tidying the rooms.

"May I come?" she begged.

"Sure," said Mary kindly. "I'm dusting the big parlor this morning, and there are lots of interesting things to see there."

In the big unused parlor she threw open the shutters and parted the curtains to let in the sunlight. Hortense was at once absorbed in the treasures she found. The room was filled with things which Grandfather had brought home from his travels all over the world. There were heavy, dark red tables carved with all kinds of flowers and animals, bright silk cushions, little ebony tabourets with brass trays upon them, curious vases and lacquer boxes from China and Japan. On the mantel was a beautiful tree of pink coral in a glass case, and beside it were wonderful shells and little elephants carved from ivory. On the walls were bits of embroidery framed and covered with glass, picturing bright-plumaged birds and tigers standing in snow.

Most fascinating of all were the strange weapons arrayed in a pattern upon one wall--spears, guns, bows and arrows, swords and knives, boomerangs, war clubs, bolos--weapons which Hortense had seen only in pictures in her geography and in books of travel. They all seemed dead and harmless enough now, not likely to come down from the wall and wander about the house at night. Hortense doubted whether they would even speak.

However, one was different, quite wide-awake and, Hortense could see, only waiting for a chance to leap down from the wall. It was a long knife with a green handle made from some sort of stone. Its shape was most curious, like the path of a snake in the dust. Like a snake, too, it seemed deadly, and the light that played upon its sinuous length and dripped from the point like water, glittered like the eyes of a serpent.

"What an awful knife," said Hortense.

"Those spears and knives give me the shivers," said Mary. "I've told your Grandfather I'd never touch them."

"Most of them are dead," said Hortense, "but the one with the curly blade and the green handle looks as though it could come right down at you. I'd like to have that one."

Mary jumped.

"Don't you touch it," she said severely. "You might hurt yourself dreadfully."

Hortense said no more, but resolved to ask Grandfather about the knife at the first opportunity. Sometime, when she had a chance, she would come to the parlor and talk with the knife. It must have lovely, shivery things to tell.

There was also a couch which fascinated her, a long, low couch with short curved legs and brass clawed feet. Hortense surveyed it for a long time.

"It looks like an alligator asleep," she said at last. "I wonder if it ever wakes up."

"What does?" Mary asked.

"The couch," said Hortense. "See its short curved legs, just like an alligator's? And it's long. Probably its tail is tucked away inside somewhere. Alligators have long tails, you know. I saw an alligator once that looked just like that."

"I declare," said Mary, "you are an awful child. I won't stay in this room a bit longer. I feel creepy."

She gathered up her dust cloths and broom, and Hortense went reluctantly with her.

"Do show me the attic, Mary," Hortense pleaded.

"Not to-day," said Mary firmly. "You'd be seeing things in the corners. I never saw your like!"

So for the rest of the morning, Mary dusted other rooms in which all the furniture seemed dead or asleep and, therefore, quite uninteresting.

After luncheon, however, Hortense asked Grandfather to tell her about the knife with the crinkly blade.

"That," said Grandfather, "is a Malay kris, such as the pirates in the East Indies carry. An old sea captain gave it to me. It once belonged to a Malay pirate. When he was captured, my friend secured it and gave it to me in return for a service I did for him."

"It looks as though it could tell terrible stories," said Hortense.

"No doubt it would if it could talk," said Grandfather. "It is very old and doubtless has been in a hundred fights and killed men."

"You wouldn't let me carry it?" Hortense asked.

"Gracious no," said Grandfather. "It is dangerous. What made you think of such a thing?"

What Hortense thought was that it would be a very nice and handy weapon to hunt the cat with at night, but she couldn't tell Grandfather that; so she said nothing.

"It's a nice afternoon," said Grandfather, "and little girls should be out-of-doors. Run out and see the barn and the orchard."

Hortense did as she was told, wandering about the yard, exploring the loft of the barn, and the orchard. At last she came back to the house, for this interested her more than anything else.

There were many bushes and shrubs planted close to the walls, forming fine secret corners in which to hide and look unseen upon the world without. Hortense hid a while in each of them, wishing she had some one with whom to play hide and seek.

She found one bush which was particularly inviting, for it was beside an open window of the basement. She looked in and was surprised to see that the window opened not into the basement but into a wooden box or chute that sloped steeply, and then dropped out of sight into the gloom below.

Hortense peered in as far as she could and as she did so, much to her surprise, a head appeared in the darkness where the wooden box dropped out of sight.

It was the head of a dirty little boy. As she stared at it, she recognized the little boy who had turned handsprings in the yard next door as she and Uncle Jonah had driven by yesterday.

"Hello," said Hortense.

"Hello," said the boy. "Help me out. I slipped."

He endeavored to lift himself to the chute whose edge came to his chin, but it was too slippery and he could not. Hortense stretched out her arm to help him, but the distance was too great.

"However did you get there?" Hortense asked.

"I wanted to see where it went," said the boy, "but once I got in I slipped and fell to the bottom."

"Where does it go?" Hortense asked.

"Only to the furnace," said the boy in disgust.

"Oh," said Hortense. "I thought it might go to a secret room or something."

"Can't you get a rope?" the boy asked.

Hortense considered.

"I couldn't pull you out if I did. I'll have to get Uncle Jonah."

"He'll lick me," said the boy.

"Oh, I know," said Hortense. "We'll play you're a prisoner in a dungeon, and every day I'll bring you things to eat."

But the boy didn't seem to like this idea.

"I want to get out," he said, and disappeared.

"I believe there's some sort of a door at the bottom," he said at last, reappearing, "but it opens from the other side. Couldn't you get into the cellar and open it?"

"Aunt Esmerelda might see me and ask what I was doing," she answered. "Maybe I can get by when she isn't looking. You wait."

"I'll wait all right," said the boy. "Don't you be too long. It's dark in here."

"The dark won't hurt you," said Hortense, but to this the boy only snorted by way of reply.

Hortense peeped cautiously into the kitchen. Aunt Esmerelda was seated in her chair, fast asleep.

"What luck," thought Hortense, and she tiptoed across the kitchen to the cellar door. She opened it very carefully, shut it again without noise, and crept down the stairs.

The basement was dark, but soon Hortense began to see her way and walked to the furnace. At the back of it was the wooden chute that led to the window above.

She knocked gently upon it.

"Are you in there?" she asked.

"Yes," said a muffled voice.

Hortense looked for the door of which the boy had spoken and at last found a panel which slid in grooves. She pulled at this but succeeded in raising it only a couple of inches.

"It's stuck," said Hortense.

"I can help," said the boy, slipping his fingers through the opening.

He and Hortense pulled and tugged and at last succeeded in raising the panel about a foot. They couldn't budge it an inch further.

"I guess I can squeeze through," said the boy.

Scraping sounds came from the box, and the noise of heels on the wooden sides. The boy's head appeared and then an arm. Hortense seized the arm and pulled.

At last a very dusty, grimy boy wriggled through and, rising gasping to his feet, dusted his clothes.

"What's your name?" Hortense asked.

"Andy. What's yours?"

Hortense told him. They looked at each other without further words.

"You've got to get through the kitchen without Aunt Esmerelda seeing you," said Hortense, and led the way to the cellar stairs.

"You stay here until I see if she's still asleep," Hortense said as she crept cautiously to the top.

She opened the door very gently and peered in. Aunt Esmerelda still sat in her corner, asleep. Hortense motioned to Andy, who came as quietly as he could, which wasn't very quiet for his heels clumped loudly on the stairs.

"Hush!" Hortense whispered. "Now go as fast and as quietly as you can across the kitchen. Hide behind the barn, and I'll follow you."

Andy ran across the room, but as he went out of the door he struck his toe against the sill, making a great clatter.

Aunt Esmerelda awoke with a start.

"Lan's sakes, wha's dat?" she exclaimed.

"May I have some cookies, Aunt Esmerelda?" Hortense asked.

Aunt Esmerelda's eyes were rolling.

"I 'clare I seed somefin' goin' out dat a doh. Dis yere house 'll be de def of me. Cookies? 'Cose you can have cookies, honey."

Hortense helped herself freely, remembering that Andy would want some. With these in her hands she walked through the yard and around the barn, where she found Andy.

"Cookies!" cheered Andy, and falling upon his share which Hortense gave him, he ate them one after another as fast as he could, never saying a word.

"Didn't you have any luncheon?" Hortense asked.

"Of course," said Andy, "but I squeezed so thin getting out of that box that I'm hungry again."

"I suppose," said Hortense, "that when I want a second helping of dessert and haven't room for it, all I need do is to squeeze in and out of the box and then I can start all over again."

It seemed a delightful plan.

"We might do it now and get some more cookies," said Andy, hopefully.

"Aunt Esmerelda would catch us and tell Uncle Jonah," said Hortense.

She meditated on the delightful possibilities of the box.

"We could play hide and seek, sometime when nobody's about," she said. "It's a grand place to hide."

"But we both know of it and there's nobody else to play with," said Andy.

This was very true unless Highboy and Lowboy and the Firedogs and Owl should be taken into the game. Hortense looked at Andy wondering whether to tell him of these friends of hers and of the Cat.

"If we played at night," said Hortense, "we could have lots of people. Highboy, and Lowboy, and Owl, and the Firedogs come out at night."

Andy stared at her with round eyes.

"They're the furniture, you know," said Hortense. "You can see some things are alive and waiting to come out of themselves. I'm sure Alligator Sofa and Malay Kris would play, too, if we asked them."

Andy's eyes were as big as saucers.

"Honest?" he asked doubtfully.

"They came out last night and we chased the cat, Jeremiah, into the attic where he disappeared," said Hortense. "We must find out where he went."

"Aw, you're fooling," said Andy, but he spoke weakly.

"Cross my heart 'n hope to die," said Hortense. "You come over to-night after everybody's asleep, and I'll show you."

"I suppose I could get out of my window all right," said Andy doubtfully, "but how could I get into your house?"

"By the cellar window and the wooden chute as you did to-day!" cried Hortense. "Then I'd unlock the cellar door, and you could come up."

Andy seemed not to like the prospect.

"It will be dark," he said.

"Oh, if you're afraid of the dark, of course," Hortense sniffed.

"Who said I was afraid?" challenged Andy.

"Well, come if you aren't afraid," said Hortense. "But you mustn't make any noise, of course, or they'll catch us."

Andy looked long at her and swallowed hard.

"I'll come," he said bravely.

CHAPTER V

"Jeremiah's disappeared again."

After dinner that night, Grandfather took Hortense on his knee and told her an exciting story, of pirates and Malay Kris.

"Is it true?" Hortense asked.

"Pretty nearly," said Grandfather. "It might be true."

"If you think things are true, then they are true, aren't they?" Hortense demanded.

"Perhaps," said Grandfather, wrinkling his forehead. "Philosophers disagree on that point. Now run off to bed."

Hortense kissed her Grandfather and Grandmother good night and went to her room.

"I hope you got a good nap to-day," she said to Highboy when she had closed the door, "because we are going to play hide and seek to-night, and Andy, who lives next door, is coming over."

"I slept all day," said Highboy, "and I'm fit as a fiddle."

"Why do you say fit as a fiddle?" asked Hortense. "Do fiddles have fits? Cats have, of course!"

"And dresses," added Highboy, "and things fit into boxes. Your grandmother says when she puts things into me, 'This will fit nicely,' so I suppose a fiddle fits or has fits the same way."

"It doesn't seem clear to me," said Hortense.

"How many things are clear?" Highboy demanded.

"Lots of things aren't," Hortense admitted. "Of course, a clear day is easy."

"And you clear the table," said Highboy.

"And clear the decks for action," said Hortense, "but that's pirates. I must ask Malay Kris about that. He's seen it happen lots of times. We'll get him to play to-night."

"Who is Malay Kris?" asked Highboy.

"He's the long, snaky knife that hangs in the parlor," said Hortense. "Then there's Alligator Sofa, too. We'll get him to play, if he'll wake up. He's so slow I suspect he'll always be *It*."

Highboy shivered until he creaked.

"They sound fierce and dangerous to me," he said, "worse than Coal and Ember."

"Perhaps we can set him on Jeremiah and the other one," said Hortense. "I'm longing to see the bright, round one with prickly sides. I've a guess as to who it is."

Highboy shivered again.

"Don't mention them in my hearing--please!" he begged. "You never can tell when Jeremiah is snooping about, and he's a telltale."

"Well, we needn't be afraid of Jeremiah," Hortense said. "Malay Kris will make the other one run, too, I expect."

She looked out of the window.

"There's no light on the lawn from the library," said she. "Everybody must be in bed. Let's go down."

"You hold my hand tight," said Highboy.

Hortense did so, and they stole down the stairs together.

Coal and Ember growled a bit when they entered Grandmother's room but stopped when they saw who it was.

"What do we do to-night?" Owl asked. "I feel wakeful."

"Andy's coming over," said Hortense, "and then we're going to ask Malay Kris and Alligator Sofa to play with us."

"Andy sounds like a boy," said Owl. "I hate boys. One robbed my nest of eggs once, and I swore I'd pull his hair if I ever met him again."

"That was another boy, I'm sure," Hortense replied.

"All boys are bad," Owl grumbled. "Who are Malay Kris and Alligator Sofa?"

"I'll show you," said Hortense, "but first I must let Andy in. The cellar door's sure to be locked. You all wait here until we come."

She found her way into the dark kitchen and, unlocking the door, stood at the head of the stairs. Soon she heard bumps in the wooden box.

"Is that you, Andy?" she called softly.

"Yes," said a muffled voice, and she heard him stumbling in the dark.

Andy found his way to the stairs at last and soon stood beside her. Hortense took him by the hand and led him to Grandmother's room.

"This is Andy," she said to the others.

"Let us smell him," said Coal and Ember, "so we'll know him in the dark."

They sniffed at his heels, and Owl glared fiercely at him.

"It's not the boy who robbed my nest," said Owl. "It's lucky for his hair."

"Now we'll go into the parlor for the others," said Hortense, leading the way.

It was so dark in the parlor that Hortense could see nothing; so she threw open the shutters, admitting a faint light which shone on Malay Kris and made him glitter.

"We want you to come down to play hide and seek," said Hortense.

"I'd rather have a fight," said Malay Kris. "It's a long time since I've tasted blood. Many's the man I've slithered through like a gimlet in a plank."

"These boastful talkers seldom amount to much," said Owl.

Malay Kris glared at Owl, whose fierce eyes never wavered.

"You have wings," said Malay Kris, "but anything that walks or swims is my meat. Show him to me."

"Nonsense," said Hortense sharply. "This is hide and seek and not a pirate ship."

"In that case," said Malay Kris, "I'll join you in a friendly game."

Down he leaped as agile as a cat, a trim, slim fellow with bright eyes.

"And now for Alligator," said Hortense. "He's asleep, as usual."

She shook him roughly, and Alligator spoke in a hoarse voice like a rusty saw.

"Who's tickling me?"

"His voice needs oiling," said Owl.

"A fat pig is what I need," said Alligator.

"Well we have no fat pigs," said Hortense. "We are going to play hide and seek."

"I'll play, of course," said Alligator, "but I'm slow on my feet. Now if it were a lake or river, I'd show you a thing or two."

"The point is, who is to be *It*? said Owl.

"Very true," said Lowboy. "He's a mind like a judge--never forgets the point."

"She's *It*, of course," said Malay Kris. "She thought of the game."

"Oh, very well," said Hortense.

"It would be more polite to make Andy *It*," said Owl. "Always be polite to ladies."

"I'll choose between Andy and me," said Hortense.

"Eeny, meeny, mona, my
Barcelona bona sky,
Care well,
Broken well,
We wo wack.

"I'm *It*. I'll count to a hundred, and the newel post in the hall will be goal."

There was a hurrying and scurrying while Hortense hid her face.

"Ready," Hortense called and opened her eyes. She moved cautiously in the dark hall and stumbled over something at the second step.

Slap, slap, slap, something went against the newel post.

"One, two, three for me," said a hoarse voice.

"That isn't fair. You slapped with your tail," said Hortense.

"Why isn't it fair?" said Alligator. "I wouldn't stand a chance with you running. Now go ahead and find the others while I take a nap."

"Well, there are plenty more," Hortense consoled herself. "I'll look in Grand-mother's room first."

The first thing she saw was the bright eyes of Owl, who was perched on the mantel.

"I see you," said Hortense and started to run back.

But Owl flew over her head and was perched on the newel post when she arrived.

"Dear me," said Hortense, "I'll be *It* all the time at this rate. I wonder if Coal and Ember are in the fireplace. She looked, but they weren't there.

"I'll try the library," thought Hortense.

She hadn't more than reached the center of the room when Coal and Ember dashed past her.

"Why didn't you tell me?" said Hortense reproachfully to the bronze image of Buddha seated placidly on his pedestal. The image didn't deign to reply.

"I wish I could make him talk," said Hortense aloud.

Somebody snickered in the corner.

"Sounds like Lowboy," said Hortense.

Lowboy started to run for the door but collided with a chair.

"I've scratched myself," said Lowboy.

Hortense did not wait to console him. Instead, she ran to the newel post.

"One, two, three for Lowboy!" she called. "Lowboy's *It*. All-y all-y out's in free."

Malay Kris crawled out from behind the clock, and the others appeared one by one.

"Lowboy's *It*," said Hortense.

Lowboy shut his eyes and began to count. Hortense seized Andy by the hand and ran with him up the stairs.

"We'll hide in the attic," she whispered.

Up and up they ran, softly opened the door to the attic, and hid behind a trunk in the corner.

"They'll never find us," said Andy.

They lay quiet and heard nothing for a long time.

"Perhaps they've given up," said Andy.

"Ssh!" Hortense whispered.

Something was running very fast up the stairs. It did not stop at the top, but raced on to the ladder which reached to the cupola above. Hortense peeped out. On the sill of the open window above stood Jeremiah with arched back and swollen tail. His yellow eyes shone like lamps.

"Of all things!" said Hortense.

Then the Cat disappeared, and they heard the soft thud of his feet alighting on the roof.

"We must see what he's up to," said Hortense.

Followed by Andy, she ran to the ladder, scrambled to the top, and peered out. The Cat was perched on top of the chimney, looking this way and that.

Hortense ducked her head in order not to be seen.

"What do you suppose he's doing there?" she asked.

"Perhaps something is after him," said Andy.

From below came a slow scratching sound. Some heavy creature with claws was coming up the attic stairs.

"Is it you, Alligator?" Hortense called.

"Where's that Cat?" said Alligator in a determined voice. "I must have him."

"He's on the roof," said Hortense, climbing down. "But what do you want him for?"

"For supper," said Alligator in his harsh voice. "He'll be furry, but eat him I will."

He started up the ladder.

"I'm old and big for such work as this," said he, "but have him I will. Push my tail a bit and give me a lift."

Hortense pushed and Andy, at the top, pulled. Out went Alligator, Hortense and Andy holding his tail while he scrambled down the roof.

Jeremiah raised his voice.

"Help! Help!" he cried as Alligator slid slowly down the roof towards him. Then, as Alligator put his forelegs against the chimney and began to lift his horrible head, Jeremiah shut his eyes and jumped.

Quick as a flash Alligator's huge jaws opened wide, and into them fell Jeremiah. Hortense could see Alligator's throat wiggle as Jeremiah went down.

Alligator crawled back slowly.

"I must seek my corner and go to sleep," said Alligator, balancing himself on the window ledge. "Hear him?"

Hortense and Andy put their ears to Alligator's back. Within they could hear Jeremiah running around and around and crying out.

"He's having a fit," said Hortense.

"A snug fit," said Alligator grimly. "He'll get used to it after a while."

Hortense and Andy were quite silent as they slowly followed Alligator down the stairs.

"It's rather horrible," Hortense whispered to Andy, "although I didn't like Jeremiah."

"I think I'll go home," said Andy.

In the hall below they found all the rest.

"Where have you been keeping yourselves?" said Owl irritably. "Ember's *It*, and we've waited ever so long."

"Alligator's swallowed Jeremiah," said Hortense.

"Served him right," said Owl, but Coal and Ember backed off as though fearing their turn would be next. Lowboy was sober for once.

"I want to go home," whimpered Highboy.

"Why didn't you let me run him through first?" demanded Malay Kris. "I'd have skewered him like a roast of beef."

"Too late," said Alligator, making off to the parlor.

"I suppose the party's broken up for to-night," said Owl.

All moved away by common consent. Hortense let Andy out of the back door and locked it after him. Taking Highboy, who was still shaking, by the hand, she led him up the stairs.

"That Alligator's a dreadful person," said Highboy. "I'm sure I'll not sleep at all."

Hortense, however, slept soundly and was late for breakfast. When she entered the dining room, Grandmother was saying, "Jeremiah's disappeared again. I wonder what can have got into him of late."

Mary, bringing toast, entered with a troubled face.

"Jeremiah's somewhere in the parlor, ma'm," she said. "I heard him crying under the sofa, but though I looked I couldn't see him. I called to him, but he wouldn't come. It's most surprising."

"We'll find him after breakfast," said Grandfather.

So after breakfast they all went to the parlor. Jeremiah's plaintive cries could be clearly heard. Grandfather looked under the sofa and poked around with a cane, but still no Jeremiah appeared.

"We'll have to move it out," said Grandfather. "He must be caught somewhere."

He moved the sofa out into the room and peered behind it. Jeremiah's cries came distinctly, but he was not to be seen.

"Most extraordinary," said Grandfather.

Aunt Esmerelda shook her head, as did Uncle Jonah.

"Dat cat is sho' a hoodoo," said Uncle Jonah.

"Something's moving in the sofa," said Hortense.

All looked, and sure enough there was a slight movement from within.

"But he couldn't get into the sofa!" said Grandmother.

Uncle Jonah and Fergus turned the sofa over on its back.

"There's no hole," said Grandfather, examining the sofa carefully from end to end, "but there is something moving inside!"

He opened his pocketknife and carefully slit the covering at one end. Uncle Jonah and Aunt Esmerelda retreated to the door and looked on with frightened faces.

Grandfather inserted his hand, felt around, and pulled forth Jeremiah, a very crestfallen cat.

"How did you get in there?" demanded Grandfather.

Jeremiah mewed and looked much ashamed.

"A most extraordinary thing," said Grandfather, carrying Jeremiah from the room.

Hortense followed with the others. As she went, she raised her eyes to Malay Kris, hanging in his customary place on the wall.

Malay Kris winked one bright eye at her.

CHAPTER VI

*"**I'll have the charm That saves from harm;**"*

Grandmother was knitting and Hortense sat on a stool at her feet, thinking, for she wished to make a request of Grandmother and she was doubtful of Grandmother's response.

"May I ask the little boy who lives next door to come in and play?" Hortense asked suddenly.

"I didn't know you had seen him," said Grandmother.

"I've seen and talked with him," said Hortense. "His name is Andy."

"You are sure that he is a nice little boy?" Grandmother asked.

"Oh yes!" Hortense cried.

"Very well, then," said Grandmother. "You may ask him to come after luncheon."

Hortense did so. After luncheon she and Andy climbed to the attic, which Hortense wished to see in the daytime, for at night she had learned very little about it.

It was a great square attic with a roof that sloped gradually to the floor from the cupola, which was like the lamp high above in a lighthouse. Like all proper attics it held old trunks, furniture, and all kinds of things. In the drawers of the bureaus and wardrobes were old suits and dresses, and in the trunks, other dresses and suits and old hangings. Andy and Hortense took them out and dressed in them--and played they were a lord and a lady, and pirates, and Indians. Then they sat down to eat the four apples which Hortense had thoughtfully brought with her.

"Where do you suppose the Cat hid the night I followed him and he disappeared?" Hortense asked.

"There are lots of corners to hide in," said Andy, but Hortense was sure that the Cat had some particular place; so Andy and she crawled all around the attic under the eaves, looking behind every trunk and into every corner. Yet they could find no place that seemed especially secret.

"There's no secret corner," said Andy, sitting down beside the big chimney and leaning his back against it.

But as he spoke he suddenly began to disappear through the floor and only by catching the edge of it did he save himself. He and Hortense were too surprised to speak for a moment. Then they knelt on the edge of the opening and peered down.

"It's a trapdoor," said Andy. "We must find out where it goes."

He pushed the door to one side and revealed a little staircase.

"Are you afraid to go down?" Andy asked.

"Of course not," said Hortense. "You go first."

Andy led the way and Hortense followed. A few steps brought them to a small room. It was dark, but the light from the trapdoor enabled them to see a little after a while. There was nothing in the room but a large chest.

"Shall we open it?" Andy asked.

"Of course," said Hortense.

By pulling and tugging they succeeded at last in lifting the lid.

"It's empty," said Andy much disappointed. "I hoped it might be full of gold and jewels."

Hortense had a sudden thought.

"This is where Jeremiah went the time we couldn't find him."

Andy was unconvinced.

"A cat couldn't open a trapdoor," he said.

"Maybe Jeremiah could. He's no ordinary cat. Besides there's another one."

"Another cat?" Andy demanded.

"No. Somebody else we haven't seen, but I can guess who it is."

"Who is it?"

"I won't tell yet--not until I'm sure. But we'll see him. Maybe we'll surprise him and Jeremiah here some night and take them captive."

"Hello," said Andy as he put his foot on the stairs. "What's this?"

Beside the chimney was a black hole and fastened to the chimney was an iron bar like the rung of a ladder. Andy peered down.

"There's another rung," he said. "I wonder where this ladder goes?"

"We'll have to find out," said Hortense. "Dear me, this is a most mysterious house."

Andy put one foot on the ladder and began to descend. Soon his head disappeared from sight.

"It goes down and down, probably to the basement," he called. "Come on."

Hortense obeyed, and down and down they went. It was very dark, but now and then a little chink beside the chimney let in a ray of light.

"Maybe it goes to the middle of the earth," said Andy from below. "No, here's the bottom at last."

Soon Hortense stood behind him. Gradually, as their eyes became accustomed to the dark, they could see a little.

"Here's the way," said Andy at last.

"But here's another passage," said Hortense.

"We'll try mine first," said Andy.

They had walked only a few steps when they came to a wooden panel.

"It's like the one that I crawled through the other day," said Andy. "Help me to move it."

It moved slowly, but finally they raised it until they could crawl through.

"I believe this is the chute I came down when you found me," said Andy.

He stood up.

"There's the basement window," he said, "and here's the little door I crawled through. Now we can get out."

"We must see where the other way goes first," Hortense reminded him.

"I'd forgotten," said Andy.

Back they went to the foot of the ladder and then down the other way which grew smaller and smaller and suddenly stopped.

"Let's go back, there's nothing here," said Hortense.

Andy stood still, absorbed in thought.

"It can't end in nothing," said he. "Who would dig a tunnel to nowhere?"

He felt the end of the passage with his hands.

"It's wood," he announced. "It must be a door. Yes, here's a little latch."

He opened the little door and, lying on his stomach, looked down the tunnel beyond. It was neatly fashioned and quite light but curved away in the distance so that the end was not visible--only a shining bit of the wall.

Hortense spoke the thought of both.

"If we were only small enough to go down it and see where it leads," said she.

But alas, it was far too small for that.

"Probably Jeremiah goes through it," said Hortense. "Where do you suppose it goes?"

"Perhaps to the middle of the earth, or to a cave filled with diamonds and gold," said Andy.

"Or maybe to the home of the fairies."

"Well, we can't know, so there's no use thinking of it."

"Still, if we watched it sometimes, we might see who goes down it," Hortense suggested hopefully, "and if it were a fairy, we might talk with him."

"We might do that," Andy agreed.

"But probably they'd know we were watching and keep hid."

They returned the way they had come, crawled through the wooden box. Into the basement, and went to the head of the cellar stairs.

"I'll see if Aunt Esmerelda is asleep," said Hortense. "If she is, we'll tiptoe across the kitchen, get some cookies, and eat them in the barn."

She opened the door cautiously and peeped in. Sure enough, Aunt Esmerelda was asleep in her chair with her apron thrown over her head. Hortense motioned to Andy and they crept quietly across the kitchen to the door, Hortense pausing a moment 'on the way to fill her pockets with cookies.

They ran unseen to the barn and climbed to the haymow where they ate the cookies. Hortense was deep in thought all the time.

"To-night," she announced at last, "we'll hide in the little room we found. You can come in by the basement window and climb up the ladder. I'll go up by way of the attic. Whom shall I bring?"

"Alligator would be too big," said Andy. "Besides, he's likely to swallow things, he has such a terrible appetite."

"And Lowboy is so fat he might get stuck going down the chimney."

"Coal and Ember are always likely to growl and give us away."

"That leaves only Owl, Highboy, and Malay Kris," said Andy.

"Owl's eyes shine so--we'd better not have him," Hortense added.

So it was agreed that that night Hortense should bring only Highboy and Malay Kris with her.

"You won't be afraid to climb the ladder all alone in the dark?" Hortense asked.

"Well," said Andy, "I'll come anyhow."

Hortense clapped her hands.

"That's just what Grandfather says to do," said she. "I wish I were brave."

"You are," exclaimed Andy.

"No, I'm not, because I have a charm. See, this little ivory monkey."

She pulled out the charm from the neck of her dress.

"While I wear this, nothing can happen to me. It's lucky."

"I don't believe in charms," said Andy.

Hortense was displeased at his doubt.

"Well, you'll see," said she.

It was nearly sundown; so Andy ran home, and Hortense returned to the house to change her dress for supper.

Said she to Highboy, "To-night you and Malay Kris and I are going to hide in the secret room in the attic. There Andy will join us, and we will watch for Jeremiah and the other."

"I do not wish to see Jeremiah or the other," said Highboy.

"Nevertheless, you must come," said Hortense firmly.

"Alas," mourned Highboy. "Never again will I stand on a good Brussels carpet and see the sunshine pour in the south window. Many a sad year shall I weep for the last embraces of my brother Lowboy and the dull life of home."

Hortense was struck to admiration by these moving words.

"How lovely," said she. "I didn't know you wrote poetry."

"I have a drawer full," said Highboy, perking up a bit.

"Then you must surely come," Hortense urged. "You might be captured, or something, and then you could be dreadfully melancholy and write the beautifullest poetry!"

"True," said Highboy. "Sorrow is the food of poets."

Consequently, when all was still and Grandfather and Grandmother were safely in bed, Highboy went willingly enough with Hortense down the dark silent stairs and past Grandmother's sitting room.

"May I not say a farewell to Lowboy?" said Highboy with tears in his voice.

"Not at all," said Hortense briskly. "He might want to come, too."

They went softly into the parlor, and Hortense whispered to Malay Kris, telling him of the night's expedition.

"Good," said Malay Kris. "If I see the Cat or the other one, I'll slither through their bones."

He spoke in a low, fierce voice and jumped down lightly so as not to awaken Alligator, who seemed to be asleep, but it was of no use. Without opening his eyes, Alligator grunted,

"Where do I come in?"

"Why, you see," said Hortense embarrassed, "you're so big you couldn't get into the little room nor climb down the ladder."

"You mean I'm not wanted," said Alligator crossly. "Very well, I'll not go where I'm not asked. I'll hunt alone."

"Dear me," said Hortense, "now he'll go and swallow something he shouldn't."

"Maybe I will and maybe I won't," said Alligator. "It depends on my appetite."

"Swallow me," said Malay Kris, "and I'll show you a thing or two. I'll run you as full of holes as a colander."

"You're not to my taste," said Alligator, yawning horribly. "If I cared to, I would."

Malay Kris glared at Alligator, but as it was of no use to attack his thick hide, which was as tough as iron, he did nothing more and Hortense dragged him away.

"Save your wrath," she said.

"I have so much I don't need to save it," said Malay Kris. "The more I spend, the more I have."

Nevertheless he came obediently enough, and Hortense and Highboy and Malay Kris climbed to the attic, went through the trapdoor, and hid in the little room. They left the door open a bit so that they could see out, and all crouched on the upper stair waiting for whatever was to come.

"What's that?" said Malay Kris. "I heard a sound."

"It's Andy, of course," said Hortense, running down the stairs. "I'd almost forgotten him."

Leaning over the hole beside the chimney, she called in a soft voice, "Andy, Andy."

"It's me," said Andy, and soon he joined them.

"Why do we wait here?" Malay Kris demanded. "How can you be sure any one will come?"

"We can't be sure, of course," Hortense said, "but it's likely because it's a secret place. We want to see who it is that goes with Jeremiah. Highboy has seen him but doesn't know his name. He's all shiny, and prickly, and hard."

"Not too hard for me," Malay Kris boasted. "I'll run him through as though he were cheese."

"It won't be so bad, once we see him," Hortense observed. "A thing is never so bad as you think it is beforehand."

"Except castor oil," said Andy. "That's worse."

They all sat in silence, waiting for something to happen.

"Unless it comes soon, I'll go out and look for it," Malay Kris growled after a time. "I rust with inaction."

"Hush!" said Hortense.

They heard the swift patter of feet on the attic stairs and across the floor.

"Only Jeremiah," Hortense whispered disappointedly, peeping out of the crack in the door. But immediately after came the clatter of metal and a bright round figure ran up the ladder after Jeremiah and disappeared through the cupola window.

Hortense clapped her hands softly.

"I knew it!" she exclaimed, full of excitement.

"What did you know?" Andy asked.

"It's the Grater! The one that hangs in Aunt Esmerelda's kitchen."

"Let me see him!" cried Malay Kris.

On the roof above their heads, light footsteps pattered rhythmically.

"I do believe they're dancing!" Hortense said.

They ran to the ladder and scrambled up.

"Careful! We mustn't let them see us," Hortense warned.

Cautiously they peeped over the window ledge. Below them on the roof, Jeremiah and Grater were dancing outrageously. The Cat pranced on his hind legs, and Grater leaped and spun like a top, so that his sides glittered in the moonlight.

"He's wearing armor," said Malay Kris. "H'm, he won't be so easy as I thought. However, I'll have a try."

Hortense laid a hand on his shoulder.

"Not now," she said. "Let's wait."

Grater began to sing in a harsh voice. As Hortense listened to the words, she hastily put her hand to her throat to make sure that the little monkey charm was safe, for it was certain the words referred to it.

I'll have the charm
That saves from harm;
The charm I'll have
And make her slave;
It's on her neck,
And I expect
She'll die of fear
When I come near.
On her I'll grate
As sure as fate.

This was certainly a disagreeable prospect, for Grater must prove very scratchy indeed.

"I surely must keep away from him," Hortense reflected.

She forgot her fear of Grater in a moment, however, for there was a noise as of claws on the attic floor, and the movement of a heavy body.

"It's Alligator!" she said aloud.

"Yes, it's me," Alligator answered. "Don't anybody try to stop me. I know that Cat's upon the roof, and I mean to have him. I'll swallow him whole."

"The Cat is dancing with Grater," said Hortense, "and Grater is a terrible person. You daren't swallow him, for he's all hard and covered with sharp points."

"I am myself," Alligator said. "I'll look him over, but it's the Cat I want. Warm and soft, he'll be."

Alligator started up the ladder, and Hortense and the others pressed aside to let him pass. Softly he slid out of the window upon the roof and was half way down it before the Cat saw him.

Jeremiah, with a howl, leaped to the top of the chimney, his back arched, his tail as large as a fox's brush.

Grater, who was a nimble fellow for all that he looked so clumsy, after one glance at Alligator ran quickly around to the other side of the roof, and Alligator, with the slow, relentless movement of a traction engine, continued after Jeremiah. Jeremiah remembered his former unhappy experience, apparently, for with one despairing meow he disappeared down the chimney. They could hear him falling slowly, his claws scratching the bricks. As he fell, his cries grew fainter and fainter. As for Alligator, he stood with his short forelegs resting on the chimney top, the picture of disappointment.

Hortense and the others were so absorbed in this interesting scene that they had quite forgotten Grater. His sudden appearance at the window so surprised them that all four slid down the ladder in a panic.

"Quick, the trapdoor!" Hortense cried.

"Let me fight him!" Malay Kris begged.

"No, no, not here!" Hortense said and pushed him before her.

Down the ladder they went as fast as they could, which wasn't very fast, for the iron rungs were slippery and Hortense had to feel for each one with her feet. Highboy was before her and once she stepped on his fingers.

"Ouch!" Highboy cried, and stopped to put his fingers in his mouth.

"Do hurry," Hortense begged, for she could hear Grater above her, already beginning to descend.

But Highboy was distressingly slow. Grater came nearer and nearer.

"Oh, dear!" Hortense said to herself, "he'll catch me in a moment and take my charm."

Then she had an inspiration. Quickly unclasping the charm, she reached down to Highboy and said, "Swallow this, quick!"

"Is it can----," Highboy began but could say no more, for she crammed it into his mouth.

"I'm sure it's indigestible," Highboy complained, "and it wasn't sweet. I don't like it."

"Hurry!" Hortense cried, for at last they were at the bottom where they could crawl through the door into the cellar.

Grater was so close that his hand was upon Hortense's foot. She jerked herself free and in a flash was up the cellar stairs and in the kitchen.

Malay Kris turned indignantly to Hortense.

"Why didn't you let me at him?" he demanded.

There was time for no further words. Grater was upon them, and Malay Kris, with a glad cry, hurled himself at his foe. It was a grand fight, but short. Malay Kris bore Grater to the floor, locked fast in a deadly embrace.

"Let me up!" said Grater in a weak, hoarse voice. "You're hurting me."

But Malay Kris, try as he might, could not do so. He had pinned his foe to the floor so securely that he, himself, was stuck fast. Andy, Highboy, and Hortense, all lent a hand but could not free him.

"Never mind," said Malay Kris, "I like the feel of this fellow and don't mind staying all night."

Whatever would Grandfather say, Hortense wondered.

There was nothing to do but leave Malay Kris to enjoy his victim. Hortense, after leading Andy out the door, ran up to her room with Highboy, who said he was too excited to sleep and that he would compose poetry all night. Hortense slept very well, however, and in the morning when she began to dress remembered her charm.

"Give me my charm, Highboy," said she.

"In the top drawer," said Highboy.

Sure enough, there it was, and Hortense fastened it hastily about her neck and ran down to breakfast, which wasn't ready.

"Aunt Esmerelda wouldn't cook breakfast this morning, and Mary is preparing it," Grandmother explained.

"Aunt Esmerelda is afraid of spooks," said Grandfather, laughing. "Indeed, I don't know how to explain it myself. What do you suppose we found this morning? That Malay kris of which I told you, that hangs in the parlor, was thrust through the grater and buried so deep in the kitchen floor that Fergus and I could hardly get it out."

Mary, bringing breakfast, announced,

"Jeremiah's shut up somewhere again. We can hear his cries but can't tell where he is."

"Not in the sofa again, I hope," said Grandfather.

"Not there," said Mary. "He sounds as if he were in the chimney."

"Impossible," said Grandfather. "But then, impossible things happen every day in this house. We'll have breakfast first, at any rate."

After breakfast Grandfather, Fergus, and Uncle Jonah found the place in the chimney where Jeremiah was caught and, knocking in a hole, let him out.

Very dirty he was, all covered with soot, and very much ashamed. He hurried away with lowered head and tail and didn't reappear until he had cleaned his coat.

Even then he would not look at Hortense, try as she would to catch his eye.

CHAPTER VII

"... there should be Little People up the mountain yonder...."

"If you will come to tea at four o'clock, Fergus will tell you a story of the Little People," said Mary to Hortense, adding as Hortense hesitated a moment, "Bring Andy with you."

Hortense accepted gladly and ran to inform Andy of the invitation and that nut cake with chocolate icing had been especially made for the occasion.

At four o'clock Andy and Hortense, in their best bib and tucker and with clean smiling faces, knocked at the door of the little cottage beyond the orchard where lived Fergus and Mary.

The tea was all that could be asked for in variety and quantity, and it was quite evident when Hortense and Andy had finished with it that if they ate even a mouthful of supper later, they would be taking a grave risk of bad dreams and castor oil.

Fergus lighted his pipe, drew his chair a little closer to the hearth, and related the story of **Shamus the Harper**.

*   *   *   *   *

You must know that a very long time ago, when many kings ruled
Ireland, there lived a boy named Shamus. He was not, however, the
son or grandson of a king, which was in itself a distinction. In
fact, his father had a bit of a farm and a few sheep, and it was
his intention that Shamus, likewise, should be a farmer and a
raiser of sheep.

Shamus, however, had other ideas. Being a shrewd lad, he saw early
that men seldom made a fortune and won the good things of the world
through toil and the sweat of their brows. Not at all! And Shamus
loved an easy life only less than he loved to play upon the harp
and sing songs of the old days, the wars of kings, and the love of
beautiful women. He was always playing upon the harp when he should
have been working in the fields and watching the sheep, and his
father soon realized that the lad was fit for no honest work but
was designed by nature only to be a harper and a maker of ballads.

One day he said to his son, "Take your harp and go to the house of
the King. Perhaps he may find a use for you, for sure it is you are
of no use to me. When you have won gold and wear fine clothes,
perhaps after long years you will return to see me in my old age,
and I will think better of you."

Shamus was glad at these words and, packing a few things in a bag
and slinging his harp upon his back, off he went to the house of
the King.

It was a fine house with many servants and poor relations of the
King, eating the bread of idleness. There were harpers, also, but

as there can never be too many of them in the world, the King said to Shamus, "Play me a ballad of kings and wars, and the love of women, and, if the song be good, you shall stay with me and have little to do but make songs and sing them."

Shamus did as he was told and sang a song which the King liked well, and accordingly the lad was given a fine coat and all he could eat and nothing to do, and he was content.

Now, the King had a daughter who was as beautiful as the dawn. No sooner had Shamus set eyes upon her than he fell in love with her and resolved to win her as his wife, if she would have him and the King would consent. He made songs which he sang to her, and the Princess liked them. She grew fond of Shamus, who was a handsome lad.

The King, however, after the way of kings and fathers, had other ideas and announced throughout the kingdom that the Princess should be the wife of him who was victorious in a quest, which was no other than to win from the King of the Little People the gold cup forever filled with good wine. No matter how much was drunk therefrom, the cup was never empty. The King chose this quest for the reason that he was very fond of good wine and could never get enough.

Shamus, therefore, like many others, set out to win the gold cup from the King of the Little People. He slung his harp on his shoulder and put a bit of bread and meat in a bag to stay him on his journey, which promised to be long.

Now, Shamus, having been reared in the country, knew that the Little People liked best to live in the hills and mountains. So to the mountains he went, making songs to lighten the long way. He made a song of running water, and of the wind in the trees, and of moonlight upon a grassy slope, and these he liked better than any songs he had yet composed.

At last he came to the hills and mountains and set himself to watch for the Little People. Every moonlight night he sat by a green hill, hoping that the Little People would come forth to dance, as is their way, but never did he chance to see them, and he began to despair of finding them. Nevertheless he was not sad, for he had his harp, and the songs which came to him were beautiful, and he cared even more for these than for the love of the Princess. One day, as he sat in the woods playing upon his harp, he chanced to look up, and there drew near a beautiful creature upon a beautiful horse from whose mane hung many silver bells that chimed sweetly in the wind.

"Play me a song if you are a harper," said she.

He played her his song of running water, and she liked it well; he played his song of wind in the trees, which she liked yet better; and then he played his song of moonlight on a grassy slope.

The beautiful creature clapped her hands.

"Come with me to Elfland," said she, "for I am Queen of that place, and I will give you a coat of even cloth and make you a minstrel at my court. Have you the courage to do so?"

"It is the one wish of my heart," said Shamus.

Accordingly, up he mounted behind the Queen of Elfland and away flew her horse, the silver bells chiming in the wind.

For three days and nights they flew, and Shamus saw the moon turn red and heard the roaring of the sea. At last they came to the Court of Elfland, where, on a golden throne, sat the King of the Little People, most brave and fierce, tugging at his beard.

"What have we here?" he roared in a big voice. "Then let him play," commanded he when the Queen of Elfland had spoken her word.

Shamus played his three songs, and the King of the Little People no longer pulled at his beard but sat as one in a dream.

"Those are good songs," said he at last. "Give him a coat of the even cloth, and he shall play to me when I desire."

Accordingly, Shamus was given a fine green coat and became a minstrel at the court of the King of the Little People. So carefree was the life, and the food and wine so good, that the memory of his former life and of the beautiful Princess became as the memory of a dim and half-forgotten sorrow, and Shamus thought no more of returning to the world.

One day, however, when he was recalling all his old songs to please the King, who, after the way of kings, was always hankering for something new, his fingers found a song of his childhood, one that carried him back to the days in his father's house. Then he also remembered other things, including the Princess and his love for her and the quest upon which he had started. His fingers fumbled with the strings, he could find no voice to sing further, and great tears rolled down his face and splashed on the ground.

"Stop it!" commanded the King of the Little People, drawing his feet up under him for fear of the damp. "Why is it you weep such wet tears?"

So Shamus told him the cause of his sorrow while the King plucked at his beard and looked wise. When Shamus had finished, the King said to him:

"If I should give you the goblet that you seek and back you should go to the world, sorrowful would be your days and nightly would you lament the lost and beautiful years you have spent with me."

"Nevertheless," said Shamus, "so it is, and I must live my life as it is ordered."

"So be it," said the King. "I do not value the goblet a whit but I must, of course, lay upon you three tasks which you must perform before it is yours."

"What are they?" Shamus asked.

"First," said the King, "get me the magic dog that belongs to the King of the Gnomes and the sound of whose silver bell drives away all thought of sorrow."

"Good," said Shamus, and away he went to seek the King of the Gnomes.

After many days and adventures too numerous to relate, he came to the house of the King of the Gnomes, which was inside a mountain and as thickset with jewels as the grass with dew on a fine morning.

Shamus told his desire and the King of the Gnomes ordered the dog to be brought. It was a tiny creature, and looking at its coat one way its color was gold, and looking at it another way its color was green, and underneath it was a fire red. Around its neck was a silver bell that chimed sweetly as it walked and at the sound of which all sorrow was forgotten.

"'Tis a fine dog," said Shamus.

"'Tis that." said the King, "and the sound of the bell is sweet, but one thing it will not do. Have you a wife?" said he.

"I have not," said Shamus.

The King looked at him long with envy in his eyes.

"Some are born lucky in this world," said he. "Know that I have a wife whose tongue is like the roar of a waterfall day and night, save now and then when she takes a nap as she is now doing. Her talk drowns out the sound of the silver bell and drives me nearly mad. Make her cease her clatter, and the dog is yours."

Just then there was a great noise and out came the Queen, talking thirteen to the dozen. The King clapped his fingers to his ears, and the magic dog put his tail between his legs and crawled under the throne. The King said never a word, but his glance said plain as day, "Isn't it as I said?"

So Shamus took his harp and began to play his song of running water. At first he could not make himself heard, but after a while, as he played, the Queen's talk came slower and slower, and softer and softer, and by and by she was speechless.

Then Shamus began to walk slowly away, and the Queen followed. On and on he walked until he came to a stream. In the middle was a stone. Around it foamed the white water. Onto the stone leapt

Shamus, still playing. The Queen stood on the bank and wrung her hands, and then with a shriek she threw herself in and was swept away in the white water.

Shamus leapt back to the bank where stood the King much pleased.

"The dog is yours," said he, "and a good bargain I've made. The silence," he said, "will be like honey on the tongue. Now and then," he said, "I'll likely come to the stream and drop in a bit of a stone. It roars louder than it did, don't you think?"

And indeed it did so, for the Queen's voice was going still and has never since stopped.

Shamus took the little dog under his arm and carried him back to the King of the Little People.

"So far so good," said the King. "Next, bring me the magic blackbird who sings so sweetly for the King of the Forest."

Off went Shamus again, this time to the forest, where he found the King sitting under an oak tree.

"What do you here?" said the King, and Shamus told him.

"I'll not part with the bird," said the King, "although I'm a bit tired of his song. It's too sweet," said he, "and I prefer the cawing of crows and the croaking of ravens. However, it is much admired by others, and therefore I shall keep him."

He ordered the bird to be brought and bade it sing, which it did most beautifully.

"His high notes are a bit hoarse to-day," said the King. "I've heard him do better."

The bird cast him a murderous glance, and Shamus, who was a singer himself, felt sore at heart that a good song should receive so little praise. However, he kept his thoughts to himself, which he had found a good practice when dealing with kings.

Also, he stayed to supper with the King and afterwards sang and played, the King every now and then breaking in with a word to say how it should be done.

"You do not badly for a beginner," said he when Shamus had finished.

Shamus could have slain him where he stood for those ungracious words, but he bided his time, pretending to be well-pleased.

When all were asleep that night, Shamus slipped from his bed and went into the woods where he began to play softly his song of the wind in the trees. Louder and louder he played, and sure enough, the blackbird soon came and perched on a tree near by. When he had done, the bird said, "It is a pleasure to hear a song well-played."

"Sorry was I to hear the words of the King when you sang so sweetly before him," replied Shamus.

"Little he knows of songs," retorted the bird, "and I'm thinking I'll go where I'll be appreciated."

"Then come with me," said Shamus. "There are kings and kings, and some are better than others."

So he told him of the King of the Little People and of the good things that came to those who sang for him.

"I'll go with you," answered the bird.

Quietly they slipped away lest the King of the Forest surprise them, and back they went to the King of the Little People.

"Good again," acknowledged the King, and he commanded the bird to sing.

"I'm almost minded to let you off the third task," the King exclaimed, "but a vow is a vow and must not be broken. Bring me last the hare that dances by moonlight."

Shamus went off a third time and traveled until he came to a fine grassy slope, and there he awaited the full moon. Sure enough, as he lay hidden, out came the hare and began to dance, leaping and bounding and playing with his shadow.

Then Shamus began to play, softly at first and then louder and louder. Higher and faster danced the hare to the music and when it was done he sat down, panting, on the grass.

"It is a good song, and never have I danced so well," exclaimed he.

"And never," said Shamus, "have I seen such wonderful dancing."

"Thank you for that," rejoined the hare. "It is not often that I get an audience which can appreciate me, and you know yourself that a bit of praise helps wonderfully to make one do his best."

"'Tis so," said Shamus. "A word of praise is meat and drink to one who sings--or dances," he added remembering the hare.

Shamus told the hare of the King of the Little People and the good things at his court.

"Belike he'd have a bit of a carrot or a patch of good clover," said the hare wistfully.

"That he would," Shamus returned heartily. "Come with me and I'll show you."

"I'll do it," said the hare, and off they went to the King of the Little People.

"You have done all that I asked," said the King, "and do you still wish to return to the world?"

"It is my fate to do so," said Shamus.

"So be it," said the King, "but long will you lament the day. It is easier to go than to return. However, I'm not saying that some day you may not come back to me, for I like you well."

The King gave Shamus the magic goblet and ordered that he be borne from Elfland, and Shamus returned to the world.

With the goblet in his pocket and his harp slung over his shoulder, he made his way to the court of the King and the Princess. On the throne sat an old woman, and the faces of those around were strange to him.

"Who are you?" she asked.

Shamus told her the story of his wanderings and produced the goblet.

"Where is the Princess?" he inquired.

At these words the old Queen upon the throne burst into loud weeping.

"Long have you been gone, Shamus," said she. "It is seven times seven years since you left me. And now I am old, and you are as you were. It is too late!"

To Shamus, the time passed in Elfland had been no more than a year, and his heart was sorrowful as he turned away without a word.

"Belike my father is dead," said he as he bent his steps toward home.

There he also found new faces and was given the word that his father had been dead this many a year. In sorrow Shamus turned away, making sad songs to comfort his heart.

Thus he wandered through the world, finding no place where he could rest. His songs were sad and all who heard them wept, but he was not unhappy, for there is a certain pleasure in even a sad song.

Yet always he longed for Elfland and the ways of the Little People, and the sound of the bell on the magic dog, whose chime brings forgetfulness of all sorrow. Try as he would, he could never find the way, and he knew that it was because his songs were sad and he was no longer young at heart.

Older he grew with white hair and feeble step, and one day he was weary and sat himself down in a wood to rest. He sat there, thinking of his lost youth and the sad ways of the world, longing to die.

As he lamented, his fingers plucked his harp and he played again his best songs, those of running water, and the sound of wind in the trees, and of moonlight on a grassy slope.

His heart grew young within him as he played, and when he rose to his feet, the dimness of age fell away from his eyes. Before him stood the Queen of the Little People, as she had stood long before.

"Will you come with me, Shamus?" said she.

"Alas," said he, "I am now too old."

"Your songs are young," said she, "and you are young again in heart. Come with me, where you may be young forever and play glad songs."

Shamus mounted up behind on the beautiful horse, away they flew, and that was the last ever seen of him upon earth.

*   *   *   *   *

Hortense and Andy sat silent a moment as Fergus looked at them with his merry blue eyes.

"I wish there were still Little People," said Hortense with a sigh.

"Perhaps there are," said Fergus. "Who knows?"

"Have you ever seen them?" Andy demanded.

"Not of late," Fergus admitted, "but when I was a young lad in Ireland I saw them many a time."

"But not here?" said Hortense.

"It's because I'm old, not because they're not about," said Fergus. "To young eyes there should be Little People up the mountain yonder on a fine moonlight night."

Andy and Hortense looked at each other as though to say, "We'll find out, won't we?" which was indeed what both of them were thinking.

CHAPTER VIII

"The sky was lemon colored, and the trees were dark red."

Uncle Jonah had declared he would trounce Andy if ever he found him in the orchard or the barn, but as Uncle Jonah was very rheumatic and had to hobble about his work, it seemed unlikely that he would ever catch Andy, who was as fleet as a squirrel. It was a fine game, however, to pretend that Uncle Jonah was "after them," and so Andy and Hortense ran and hid whenever Uncle Jonah came in sight.

One afternoon they were seated in the grape arbor enjoying the early grapes, which were forbidden, when Uncle Jonah suddenly appeared. The only way to escape was through the vines and lattice, a tight squeeze, and Uncle Jonah nearly had them.

"I seed yo'," Uncle Jonah called, "an' I's gwine tell yo' Gran'pap."

Andy and Hortense ran as if possessed. Into the barn they went and up into the haymow where they were usually safe, but as they lay panting on the hay, Uncle Jonah entered the barn, grumbling to himself.

Andy and Hortense lay as still as mice. Uncle Jonah was with the horses. They could hear the slap of his hand upon their fat backs and his, "Steady now, quit yo' foolin'."

"Done et all yo' hay, have yo'? Spec's dis po' niggah to climb dose staihs and tho' down some mo'? I ain't gwine do it, no suh."

Nevertheless, soon Andy and Hortense heard Uncle Jonah's step on the stairs and they gazed at each other in fright.

"Where shall we hide?" Hortense gasped.

"Slide down the hay chute and into the manger," said Andy quickly. "The horses won't bite, and we can get away before Uncle Jonah comes down."

In a moment they were at the chute and, holding to the edge, dropped down, Andy first and Hortense on top. Andy scrambled through the hole into the manger and Hortense after him, but the hole was small, and Hortense plump, and it was only by hard squeezing that she got through at all.

Once in the manger, it was only a moment before they were out from under the velvety noses of the horses and had slipped past them through the stall. They ran out of the barn and to the kitchen where they secured an unusually large supply of cookies; then hurried to the nook in the shrubbery beside the basement window that led to the furnace, a good place to hide.

They ate cooky for cooky until they had eaten ten apiece, when they stopped to rest a bit. Hortense was still warm and unbuttoned her collar. As she did so, she was conscious of missing something and felt again carefully.

"I've lost my charm," she said hurriedly.

"Perhaps it slipped down inside," Andy suggested.

Hortense felt of herself but could not find it.

"I must have lost it going down the hay chute," she said. "I know I had it in the haymow. It must have come off when I squeezed through. Dear me, if I should lose it!"

"We'll find it when Uncle Jonah goes away from the barn," Andy consoled her.

They attacked the remaining cookies.

"I wonder how many cookies I could eat," said Andy dreamily as they began their thirteenth.

"I've had most enough," said Hortense taking another bite.

Then she began to feel very strange. Everything about her seemed to grow larger and larger, except Andy. The entrance to the basement seemed as wide as the barn door; the lilac bush over her head looked as big as an oak tree, and the piece of cooky in her hand as big as a dinner plate.

"What's happened to us?" Andy asked.

"I believe," said Hortense, "that we've grown small, or everything else big. I don't know which."

"How'll we ever grow big again?" Andy asked.

"We won't worry about that now," said Hortense practically. "It'll be lots of fun to be small. We can hide so nobody can find us and surprise people. I believe I could climb right into one of Highboy's drawers, or even into the jar where Grandpa keeps his tobacco."

"Mother'll never be able to find me when she wants me to weed the garden," said Andy hopefully.

Hortense's eyes grew wide, and she looked at Andy with a great idea in her eyes.

"What is it?" Andy asked.

"Now we can go through the little door and down the shining tunnel!" said Hortense.

It was so bright an idea that they wondered they hadn't thought of it sooner.

"But we're so small, how'll we ever get to the bottom of the chute? It'll be twice as high as we are."

Hortense hadn't thought of this difficulty.

"We can't go through the kitchen either, for we might be seen," said she. "Besides, the kitchen steps would be too high for us."

Andy was thinking.

"If we could find a long enough stick, we could carry it with us; then we could slide down it. After that it would be easy."

So they hunted for a stick and finally found one that looked as if it would do, but it was all they could do to get it into the basement opening. Once in, however, it was easily pulled down the chute to the edge of the drop below. Andy and Hortense lowered it carefully until the end rested on the bottom.

"Hooray," said Andy. "It's long enough."

And climbing onto it, he slid down and was soon out of sight.

"All right," he shouted a moment later, "I'm down."

Hortense then took hold, and with Andy steadying the stick at the bottom, she soon slid down and stood behind him.

Hand in hand they ran down the dark passage that led to the little door. It seemed a long way, and when they arrived, the little door seemed as big as any ordinary door. Andy pulled at the latch and swung it open, and there before them was the shining tunnel that curved out of sight. They stood a moment looking at it.

"Where do you suppose it goes?" Andy asked.

"It must go to the Little People," said Hortense. "Nobody else could use it."

"We'll find out, at any rate," said Andy, and together they ran down it.

It curved and curved and grew brighter and brighter as they ran, always a little downhill.

"I believe there's no end to it," said Hortense after they had gone what seemed a long way.

"There must be," said Andy. "Why I believe this is the end, and it's raining."

They came into what seemed to be a large cave whose roof was high above them, and from the roof water was dripping as fast and as thick as rain. The cave was as bright as moonshine and the drops sparkled as they fell. Through the falling drops, far on the other side of the cave, they saw a bright opening like the one through which they had come.

"We must run across," said Hortense, and hand in hand they dashed through the rain and into the little tunnel which was just like the one they had left, except that it began to slope up instead of down and soon was quite steep. As they paused for breath after climbing a long distance, Hortense, who had been thinking hard, said to Andy, "Do you know, I believe the cave with the falling water was under the brook, and now on this side we are going up the inside of the mountain."

"Perhaps we will come out in the cave where the Little People live," said Andy. "At least Fergus thinks they live there."

They hurried on, hoping that Andy's guess might be right, but when at last they reached the end of the passage and unlatched a little door exactly like that through which they had entered, they came out neither upon the mountain side nor in a cave, but in a strange country such as they had never seen before. The sky was lemon colored and the trees were dark red.

Before them, in the distance, was a little house with a steep roof and a pointed chimney. As they drew closer, they saw two windows in the end, set close together like a pair of eyes. Andy and Hortense walked slowly towards it, hand in hand. It was in a little garden surrounded by a hedge of cat-tails and hollyhocks.

"I never saw a hedge of cat-tails before," said Andy, and indeed it looked very odd.

There was a little gate, and through it Andy and Hortense entered the garden.

Nobody was to be seen nor was there any sound. Andy and Hortense, coming closer, peeked through a window. They could see a fire on the hearth and a tall clock in the corner, but no person was visible.

"Let's go in." said Andy, and Hortense, agreeing, followed him around the corner to a little door which was unlatched.

Nobody was in the room, which had three chairs, a table, the clock which they had seen through the window, and in the corner a great jar, taller than they were, with **Cookies** printed in large letters on the outside.

"Dear me, what a large cooky jar," said Hortense. "I'd like to look in."

But Andy could not reach the top to remove the cover, try as he would. He stood on a chair to do so and though he could now reach the cover, it was too heavy for him to budge.

Hortense, meanwhile, was looking about her to see what she could see, and as she did so her eyes fell on something familiar. In a glass case on the mantel was the monkey charm which she had lost in the barn. Hortense examined it closely to be sure that it was the same. Yes, there was the very link in the chain which she had noticed before because it was more tarnished than the others--and there was a broken link. She must have caught it as she slipped through the hay chute into the manger.

Hortense tried to reach the glass case but could not. She stood on a chair, but there was no apparent way of removing the glass. Tug as she and Andy might, the glass would not move.

"We might break the glass," Andy suggested.

"You cannot break it," said the old Clock suddenly.

"Why, it's exactly like our clock at home!" said Hortense. "I believe it's the same one. However could it have gotten here?"

"Time is the same here and everywhere, now and forever," said the Clock. "You cannot get away from time."

"Time isn't the same," said Hortense. "There are slow times and times when everything goes fast."

"It's only because you think so," said the Clock. "I go precisely the same at all times."

"When I'm asleep, where does time go?" Hortense asked. "The night goes in no time."

"Of course, in no time things are different," said the Clock. "I was speaking of time, not of no time."

Hortense puzzled over this, for it didn't seem right somehow.

"Well, no matter about that," said Hortense. "Tell us whose house this is--that's the important thing just now."

"Couldn't you tell whose house it is by looking at it?" asked the Clock. "I should think anybody could."

"It looks like something I've seen before," said Hortense, "but I can't remember what."

Then suddenly she did remember.

"It's the Cat's house!" said she. "And it has my charm!"

"Just so," said the Clock. "If I were you, I'd go away at once."

It seemed excellent advice, and Andy and Hortense turned to obey, but as they did so, in walked Jeremiah, a Jeremiah that seemed as big as a lion.

"Well, well," said Jeremiah in a purring voice, "if this isn't Andy and Hortense. I didn't think I'd find you here. How small you've grown!"

"I didn't look to find you here," said Hortense severely, "You should be at home where you belong."

But Jeremiah only smiled at this and yawned, showing his great sharp teeth. Then he stretched and sharpened his claws on the floor. His claws tore up great splinters with a noise like that of a sawmill, and Andy and Hortense were very much frightened.

"Let us past," Hortense said in a brave voice which trembled a little.

Jeremiah only blinked his great green eyes and smiled a little, very unpleasantly.

Hortense and Andy looked at the windows, but these were fastened tight, and Jeremiah, besides, was looking at them from his lazy green eyes.

"Don't go just yet," Jeremiah purred in a voice that shook the house. "It wouldn't be polite to hurry away. Besides, my friend Grater would be disappointed."

Andy and Hortense, being now but ten or twelve inches tall, had even less wish to see Grater than formerly. Hortense was aware of a sinking feeling in her stomach.

The door flew open and in walked Grater, and very large and rough he looked. Where Malay Kris had run him through, he wore a large patch of pink court-plaster. His eyes fell upon Andy and Hortense and a wide and wicked smile appeared upon his unhandsome countenance.

"Well, well," said Grater in his rough voice, "if here aren't our little friends. We must urge them to stay with us. Jeremiah, put these nice plump children in the cooky jar for future use."

With two steps Grater was across the room, and he removed the cover of the jar.

"In with them, Jeremiah," said Grater, and Jeremiah, rising lazily, took first Andy and then Hortense by the collar and dropped them into the jar. The top came down with a clatter, and Hortense and Andy were in the dark.

The jar was empty and the sides were smooth as glass.

"Stand on my back," said Andy, "and see if you can reach the cover."

Though Hortense could just reach it, it was far too heavy for her to move.

"It wouldn't be of any use," said Hortense. "They'd catch us again even if we did get out."

So they sat quiet for a long time. Hortense felt like crying, but managed not to. After a time she became hungry and put her hand in her pocket. There was a large piece of cooky which she had put there when she began to grow small and had completely forgotten.

"I have a piece of cooky," said she, breaking it in two and giving Andy half.

"If we eat any more, we may grow still smaller," said Andy.

"I don't care, I'm hungry," said Hortense. "Besides, if we grow very small perhaps the Cat won't see us when he looks into the jar--or we'll be too small to eat, at any rate."

It seemed a slim chance, but Hortense took a bite of cooky and waited to see what would happen.

"I'm not growing smaller," said she. "I do believe I'm growing bigger!"

She stood up quickly.

"I can reach the top," said she.

Andy stood up, too.

"I'm still growing," said Hortense. "Quick. We must get out before the jar is too small for us, or we'll be squeezed in and can't get out."

Together they pushed as hard as they could. The top of the jar fell off with a loud crash and Andy and Hortense scrambled over the edge, just in time, for they were growing bigger very fast.

The room was empty and dark except for the fire on the hearth.

"Hello," said the Clock, "is it you again? Better run while you have a chance!"

Andy and Hortense obeyed without a word, and hand in hand they ran through the door, into the garden, and out of the gate.

"We can't go back the way we came," said Hortense, panting, after they had run a long distance. "We're too big now."

"There must be another way out," said Andy.

So they ran on and on, through the trees.

"What a funny light it is," said Hortense, stopping at last and looking up. "I do believe the moon is blue here."

So it was--a blue moon in a lemon colored sky.

"I've heard of blue moons," said Hortense. "They must be very rare."

"They're rather nice," said Andy, "but I suppose we'd better not linger."

"Here's a path," said Hortense.

They ran along the path, which grew darker and darker, until they came to a gate on which was a sign printed in large letters. By peering close, Andy and Hortense could just make out the words:

PRIVATE PROPERTY
NO TRESPASSING

"We have to go through, whosesoever it is," said Hortense, determinedly, and unlatching the gate through they went.

The path grew darker and smaller, walled on each side by rock. Soon they had to crawl on their hands and knees.

"I don't believe we can get out this way," Hortense said at last.

"Yes, we can," said Andy, who was in front. "I see light ahead."

Sure enough, out they soon came into yellow moonlight, such as they had always known. They were upon a large flat rock. Below them was a steep tree-covered slope, and at the bottom lights twinkled.

"It's the side of the mountain," said Hortense, "and that's the house way down there. How'll we ever get there?"

"We'll have to go down the mountain side," said Andy. "Do you know," he added, "I believe this is the very spot which Fergus pointed out to us? Maybe the Little People come here. Shall we hide and see?"

"Let's," agreed Hortense.

They hid in the shadow of a tree by the edge of the rock and waited, not making a sound.

The moon rose higher over the mountain until the rock was almost as light as day, but still no one appeared.

"Let's go home," said Hortense at last in a sleepy voice.

But Andy, who was listening with alert ears, whispered.

"Hush, I hear something."

Hortense, too, listened and at last heard a faint sweet sound from within the mountain. Nearer and nearer it came, to the very mouth of the cave. Then appeared a band of Little People in green coats and red caps, each with a white feather at the side.

They marched slowly, a band of musicians at the head playing upon tiny instruments which made high, sweet music no louder than the shrilling of gnats. Following the musicians came the King and Queen with little gold crowns on their heads and wearing robes with trains borne by pages. Then came eight stout fellows carrying two golden thrones which they placed on a little eminence.

The King and Queen seated themselves, and the fairy band, after marching once around the rock, formed in a hollow circle. The King clapped his hands and rose, whereupon the musicians ceased playing, and there was complete silence. The King was taller than the others by half a head; his beard was long and tawny, and his presence royal. Said the King:

"The moon is high and the night still. It is a fitting time and place for our revels. Let the musicians play."

The musicians struck up a slow stately dance, and the King, taking the Queen by the hand, advanced to the middle of the circle and with her stepped a minuet. When the music ceased, all the Little People clapped their hands in applause, and the King and Queen reseated themselves, smiling graciously.

"The rabbit-step," commanded the King, and immediately the musicians began so lively a tune that Andy and Hortense found it difficult not to join in, which would have spoiled everything. At once, all the Little People began to skip like rabbits, in the moonlight. Around and around they went, dancing like mad, and Hortense and Andy grew dizzy watching them.

Again the music changed, and the Little People danced a square dance, after which they formed in rings within rings and whirled around faster and faster until they seemed only rollicking circles of green in which not one face could be distinguished from another.

A shadow as of a cloud fell upon the dancing Little People, and Hortense, looking up, saw what seemed to be a dark spot on the moon. Larger and larger it grew until she could distinguish it to be a pair of horses ridden by figures only too familiar.

"It's Jeremiah and Grater!" she whispered to Andy.

The fairy King had also seen. Suddenly he clapped his hands and the music and dancing ceased.

"Away!" the King shouted, and in a twinkling not a fairy was to be seen. The shadow grew larger and larger until it wholly obscured the moon. Then in a twinkling the horses came to earth and stood panting, with drooping heads.

"Why, it's Tom and Jerry!" said Hortense to herself, being careful not to make a sound.

Jeremiah and Grater dismounted.

"Well," said Jeremiah lazily, "I was sure we'd never catch them this way. You'll have to lie in wait and pounce on them."

"You and your mousing tricks!" said Grater contemptuously.

But Jeremiah only yawned.

"There's a cooky jar at home with something in it," he reminded Grater. "Let's go."

With a bound Jeremiah and Grater mounted their weary steeds, and in a moment they were out of sight over the tree tops.

"Did you ever!" exclaimed Hortense.

"I think we'd better go home," Andy suggested.

Accordingly, they struck down the steep mountain side and soon were at the foot, where ran the brook.

"We'll have to wade," said Andy.

They plunged in and across, and with wet shoes and stockings, ran across the pasture, through the orchard to the house.

"It's late. Whatever will they think!" said Hortense.

"I'm going straight to bed without being seen," said Andy.

It seemed the only thing to do, so Hortense stole quietly in and up the dark stairs to her room.

"Where have you been?" Highboy demanded when she had shut the door. "You've been looked for everywhere."

Hortense was too sleepy to reply, and in the morning no one questioned her, for Uncle Jonah had a sorry tale to tell of the horses, who lay in their stalls too tired to move, their manes and tails in elflocks, and their flanks mud stained.

"Dey's hoodooed," said Uncle Jonah, shaking his head.

To this, Grandfather made no answer but looked puzzled, and Hortense, who could have told him how it all happened, didn't know how to begin; so said nothing.

CHAPTER IX

"Tell us a story about a hoodoo, Uncle Jonah,"--

Andy had driven Tom and Jerry in from the upper pasture for Uncle Jonah, who was forced to admit that Andy wasn't so bad a boy as he had thought. It seemed a good time, therefore, to ask Uncle Jonah about the hoodoo.

"What is the hoodoo, Uncle Jonah?" Hortense asked.

"How come yo' 'quire 'bout dat?" Uncle Jonah asked. "Ah dunno nuffin' 'bout no hoodoo."

"You said Tom and Jerry were hoodooed," said Andy and Hortense together.

"Jes' foolish talk," said Uncle Jonah.

"Tell us a story about a hoodoo, Uncle Jonah," Hortense begged.

"Ah don' know nuffin' 'cept about Lijah Jones an' old Aunt Maria," said he at last.

"Tell us that," said Andy and Hortense together.

Uncle Jonah put a coal from the fire in the palm of his hand, and while Andy and Hortense watched breathlessly to see whether he would burn himself, he slowly lighted his corncob pipe. Then he began.

*   *   *   *   *

One mawnin' dis yere Lijah Jones was a-traipsin' along when he met Aunt Maria.

"Mawnin'," says Lijah, keerless like, "yo' been a hoodooin' any one lately, Aunt Maria?"

Dis yere Aunt Maria, she got a bad name and Lijah know it. Aunt Maria, she stopped an' looked kinder hard at Lijah.

"Huh," she says, "Don' yo' fool wid me, niggah."

Lijah, he step along faster, not sayin' nothin' but feelin' kinda oneasy. He wisht he ain't said dem words.

Dat evenin' Lijah come back fum town wid some co'n meal an' a side o' bacon. As he come thu de woods by Aunt Maria's cabin, he kinda shivered 'cose it wuz gettin' late an' de owl wuz a-hootin'. Dey wan't no light in Aunt Maria's cabin, but dey wuz a little fiah in de back yah'd, an' Lijah, he seed some one a-stoopin' ovah it. Lijah wuz dat curyus he crep' roun' de co'nah of de cabin an' stuck his head out. Sho'nuf, dey wuz Aunt Maria a-stirrin' a big black pot an' a-croonin' somefin' dat make Lijah tremmle lak a leaf. He don' make out wat she say 'cept, "Hoodoo Lijah Jones."

Dat was 'nuf, an' Lijah, he crep' away quiet an' hurry home thoughtful-like. He don' believe in no hoodoo, but he wuz oneasy. Dat night he say nuffin' 'bout it to his wife, but he go to bed early.

Bambye he wake up. Dey wuz a kinda noise goin' on by de ba'n, but Lijah, he ain't got no likin' fo' to get up an' see wat's de mattah. So he tu'n ovah, an' bambye he ain't heah no mo' noise, an' he go to sleep ag'in.

In de mawnin' w'en he go to milk de cow, sho'nuf dey wuz a hawg a-lyin' on its side, daid. Lijah, he scratch his haid an' tu'n de hawg ovah wid his foot. He don' know what happened to it, but he kinda s'picioned.

De nex' day w'en he wuz a-goin' down de road, 'long comes Aunt Maria ag'in.

"Mawnin'," says Aunt Maria.

"Mawnin'," says Lijah, kinda scaihed-like.

Dat was all dey said. Aunt Maria, she laugh an' go 'long, an' Lijah, he don' lak de soun'.

Dat night nuffin' happen, an' Lijah, he feel bettah. But de nex' night Lijah wake up ag'in an' heah somefin', an' sho'nuf in de mawnin' bof his mules wuz dat wo'n out lak dey been a-runnin' in de mud all night, dat he cain't do no wuk wid 'em.

Lijah, he kinda desprit wid dis, an' so dat night he don' go to bed but sit up an' hide in de ba'n. Sho'nuf, 'bout twelve o'clock 'long comes somefin', an' quicker'n nothin' bof dem mules wuz out'n dey stalls an' away down de road. Lijah, he reckon he seed somefin' a-ridin' em, an' he know mighty well wat it wuz.

In de mawnin' bof de mules was back ag'in, wo'n out, wid dey eahs droopin', and ag'in Lijah, he cain't do no wuk.

Dat night he don' set up 'cose 'tain't no use. But he wek' up sudden an' heah somefin' a-sayin', "Go to de ole house by de swamp and mebbe yo' fin' somefin'."

In de mawnin' he membah wat he heah an' he feel brave an' sco'nful, but dat night he don' feel so brave 'cause he knowed 'bout dat house. Nobody live in it but ha'nts, an' he don' like ha'nts nohow.

Howsomevah he made up his min' t'go, an' 'bout nightfall he fin' his way to de ole house by de swamp. It mighty lonely deh and Lijah, he tremmle a bit. He strike a match an' look 'roun'. On de table dey wuz a lamp, an' Lijah, he light de lamp an' feel a heap bettah.

Den he set deh a long time, an' all he heah wuz de hootin' of de owls and de crickets a-chirpin' in de grass. Lijah, he drowse a bit. Bambye he open his eyes an' deh, across de table, wuz a big black cat a-settin' an' lookin' at him.

Lijah, he don' say nothin' an' de cat say nothin', jes' look outa' his big green eyes. Bambye de lamp, it go down an' den it flame up bright, an' Lijah, he look at de cat an' he think it biggah dan befo'. De cat, it riz up and stretch an' it seem powahful big.

Lijah, he riz up, too.

"What fo' yo' goin'?" say de cat.

"Ah bleeged to go home," say Lijah, an' he out's thu dat doh quicker'n nothin' wid de cat aftah him. Lijah, he run fo' his life. Bambye he catched up wid a rabbit a-lopin' along.

"Outa' my way, rabbit," sez Lijah, "an' let somebody run wat kin run."

An' all de time dat cat kep' right aftah him, an' he mos' feel its claws on his back.

Lijah was nigh wo'n out w'en he come to his house. He opens the doh quick an' slams it shut; den he heahs de cat a-scratchin' on de doh an kinda' sniffin' 'bout, an' Lijah, he lays down on de bed plumb wo'n out.

In de mawnin' he tell his wife all 'bout it. She sez nothin' fo' a while but jes' set a-figgerin'. Den she sez, "Yo' one fool, niggah. Go an' kill de bes' hawg an' cut him up. Den yo' take one side to Aunt Maria an' be mighty perlite."

Lijah, he don' like dis nohow, but he done what his wife tole him. He tote dat side of hawg to Aunt Maria, an' she smile wicked when she see him comin'.

"I brung yo' a side of nice hawg what I jes' kill't," says he perlite.

"I sho's mighty bleeged," sez Aunt Maria. "I kin use a bit of hawg meat. An' how is yo' gittin' 'long?"

"Not very good," sez Lijah. "Ah don' seem to have no luck."

"Mebbe yo' luck will change," says Aunt Maria, smilin'-like.

An' sho'nuf, Lijah, he don' have no bad luck no mo'. But he wuz allays perlite aftah dat, an' he don' say nothin' disrespectfu' 'bout hoodoos an' ha'nts.

*　　*　　*　　*　　*

Hortense sat thoughtfully.

"We don't know anybody to give anything to because of Tom and Jerry," said she.

Uncle Jonah moved uneasily.

"I reckon we jes' gotta wait an' see whut happens," said he. "I don' know nothin' 'bout it, an' I ain't gwine mix up wid it. Yo' tek my advice and keep clear uv 'em."

CHAPTER X

"Ride, ride, ride For the world is fair and wide."

Andy and Hortense were planning what they should do next, for it was certain that they must go back to the Cat's house and secure the monkey charm, if they could. Also, they wished very much to see the Little People again, dancing on the rock in the moonlight.

"If we hide in the barn, perhaps we can see Grater and Jeremiah ride away on Tom and Jerry," said Hortense.

"But what good will that do?" Andy asked.

"Let's take every one along--Alligator, and Malay Kris, and Highboy, and Lowboy, and Coal and Ember, and Owl. Perhaps we'll think of something. Or maybe Alligator will swallow Grater!"

"It doesn't do any good for Alligator to swallow anything," said Andy. "It's always found in the sofa in the morning anyhow."

"Grandfather might know what to do with it," said Hortense. "And perhaps it would go away."

Andy had nothing better to propose and so it was agreed to do as Hortense suggested. That evening, when all was dark and silent, Hortense gathered every one in the parlor and told them the plan.

"It doesn't sound very definite," Owl grumbled.

"Suggest something then," said Hortense sharply.

But Owl only looked wise and said nothing.

Hortense found it quite difficult to hide all her companions in the barn. Owl, because his eyes were so bright, was made to go up in the loft and look down through a knot hole in the floor; Highboy and Lowboy, hand in hand, stood behind a door; Coal and Ember crouched in a corner, and Hortense told them that if they growled she would never take them out again. Alligator merely lay on the floor and, unless one looked close or felt his rough skin, one would never have guessed who he was. Malay Kris, who was slim and not easily seen, crouched beside the stalls, and Andy and Hortense covered themselves with some old empty sacks beside the wall where they could see and not be seen.

They lay hidden a long time, and nothing happened. Now and then some one moved or made a little noise, and Hortense said, "Hush!" After that they would remain quiet for a time.

The moon rose late, and its light slowly crept across the floor until it fell upon Malay Kris, who moved a little way into the shadow again. Andy and Hortense, under the old sacks, were uncomfortably warm and very stiff from lying so long in one position.

"I don't believe they are going to come at all," said Hortense in a low voice to Andy.

"Doesn't look like it," agreed Andy.

Then they lay quiet again.

Suddenly they heard a squeal from behind the barn. It made Hortense jump.

"It's only one of the pigs," Andy whispered.

Alligator had heard, too. They saw him raise his head; then slowly crawl towards the door.

"Come back!" Hortense commanded in a fierce whisper.

But Alligator paid no heed. He crawled through the doorway and disappeared.

"I'll never bring him again," Hortense whispered, much vexed. "He's always doing things he shouldn't and getting us into trouble."

She had no sooner said the words than another quick squeal came from behind the barn, and then silence.

"He's swallowed the pig," said Andy.

It seemed probable, indeed, that he had done so, but they saw no more of Alligator and didn't dare go out to look for him.

Hortense must have taken a brief nap after that, for suddenly she became aware of Jeremiah standing in the doorway. He had come so quietly that she hadn't heard him at all.

He stood there a moment, his back arched and his tail waving--his great green eyes roving about the barn. Then, with a tiny sound, appeared Grater. Tom and Jerry, in their stalls, began to tremble. Grater laughed unpleasantly and chanted in a rough voice:

Ride, ride, ride
For the world is fair and wide.
The moon shines bright
On a magic night,
And Tom and Jerry
Are able very
To ride, ride, ride.

With one bound Grater and Jeremiah were on the backs of the horses, and in a twinkling the horses were out of their stalls and running toward the door. Quick as they were, Malay Kris was almost as swift. In a flash he hurled himself at Grater, grazed him, and stuck deep in the wall, where he quivered and grew still.

"Missed!" Malay Kris said bitterly.

Andy and Hortense, with open mouths, watched the horses and riders grow smaller and smaller against the moon, and finally disappear.

"Did you ever!" Hortense gasped at last.

Hortense and Andy crawled out from under their sacks and found the rest of their band. Highboy and Lowboy, hand in hand, were leaning against the wall, fast asleep, and had seen nothing at all. Hortense shook them vigorously to awaken them.

"You're a pretty pair," she said.

"Thank you," said Lowboy, "Our beauty is due to contrast. We set each other off. He is tall and graceful, and I am short, and round like a ball. Some think me handsomer than he."

Hortense turned her back upon him.

"I'm out of patience with you," she said disgustedly.

Lowboy's mouth began to droop at the corners; his eyes closed and round tears, like marbles, began to roll down his cheeks. Highboy hastened to offer him a hand-kerchief.

"You musn't cry, you know," said Highboy, "or you'll warp yourself--maybe even stain your varnish."

"Then I'll abstain," said Lowboy, and was so pleased with his pun that he at once began to laugh.

Hortense, however, was still out of temper, quite unreasonably, because she couldn't really think of anything which any one should have done.

"Where were you, Coal and Ember?" she demanded severely.

"In the corner where you put us," Coal and Ember growled with one voice.

"Why didn't you do something?"

"Take a bite out of Grater?" Coal suggested sarcastically. "You can't bite any-thing that hasn't a smell!"

"Why can't you?" Hortense inquired sharply.

"Because if it hasn't any smell it hasn't any taste, and how can you bite a thing if you can't taste it?"

"You mean, how can you taste it if you don't bite it," said Hortense.

"I mean what I say," said Coal.

"How doggedly he speaks," said Lowboy, who burst into loud laughter. Nobody else laughed, and Lowboy explained his joke. "Dog, doggedly, see?"

"It's a poor joke," said White Owl, flying down the stairs.

"Make a better one then," said Lowboy.

"I never joke," said Owl. "None of our family ever did."

"So that's what's the matter with them all," said Lowboy. "I always wondered--or should I say I *owlways* wondered?"

"That's really a good joke," said Ember. "I didn't suppose you had it in you."

"It isn't in me," said Lowboy. "If it were in me, you couldn't have heard it."

"It *was* in you or it couldn't have come out," said Ember.

Hortense stamped her foot.

"Oh do hush, all of you," she said. "The trouble with you all is that you talk and talk and do nothing. Only Malay Kris says little and acts."

"And look what happens to him," said Owl.

Malay Kris did, indeed, look uncomfortable, half buried in the wall, but he endeavored to be cheerful.

"Some one will rescue me in the morning," he said. "I shouldn't mind at all if I'd tasted blood."

"Instead you only struck the air," said Lowboy. "You must be an Airedale like Coal and Ember."

Nobody laughed.

"It's no use making jokes for such an unappreciative audience," Lowboy grumbled. "Take care, Kris, that you don't get wall-eyed during the night."

Still nobody laughed.

"Surely you get that one!" said Lowboy. "It's very simple--wall, wall-eyed, you see."

"I appreciate you," said Highboy, "but you know I never laugh."

"You'd grow fat if you did," said Lowboy. "Speaking of fat, let's see what's happened to Alligator. Three guesses, what has he done?"

But nobody guessed because they were all quite sure what Alligator had done. They went out in a body to look for him. He lay beside the barn with his eyes shut and a smug smile on his face. Muffled grunts and squeals sounded from his inside.

"What good does it do to eat things when you have to give them up in the morning?" Hortense asked.

"What good does it do you to eat supper when you have to eat breakfast in the morning?" demanded Alligator.

"It isn't the same thing," said Hortense.

"It's meat and cake and milk at night, and oatmeal and toast in the morning," said Lowboy. "Not the same thing at all."

"That isn't what I mean," said Hortense.

"Well, say what you mean then," said Owl sharply.

"You are all very disagreeable to-night," announced Hortense.

"Let's vote for the most disagreeable person," said Lowboy. "I nominate Hortense. Are there any questions? If not, the ayes have it and Hortense is elected."

Hortense was so angry that she walked away and would hear no more. Nor did she even wait to see that Alligator returned to the parlor.

In the morning as she lay in bed, she wondered if he had and, dressing herself quickly, ran outdoors to see. As she ran around the barn, she came upon Grandfather and Fergus looking at the sofa. Grandfather was stroking his chin.

"How could it possibly have got here?" said he. "All the doors and windows were locked as usual this morning."

"Well, who would carry it out and leave it in such a place, anyhow?" said Fergus.

A slight movement which stirred the seat of the sofa caused them all to gaze at it wonderingly. Then a sound came from within.

"The second time!" exclaimed Grandfather. "If it's the cat again, I'll know he's the cause of all these odd doings."

"It didn't sound like a cat to me," said Fergus.

Grandfather, without a word, opened his penknife. Fergus and he turned the sofa over, and Grandfather slit the under covering where it had been sewed up after Jeremiah had been rescued. Through the hole appeared the head of a pig. Grandfather and Fergus stood back while the pig struggled to free himself. Finally succeeding, it trotted away to its pen.

Grandfather and Fergus looked at one another, at first too surprised to speak.

"Do you suppose," said Grandfather at last, "that the pig got into the sofa and carried it off, or the sofa came out and swallowed the pig?"

"I give up," said Fergus, scratching his head.

Grandfather pondered a while and then looked at Hortense.

"It's a curious thing, Fergus, but all these things began to happen when Hortense came. Do you suppose she is responsible?"

He looked so grave that Hortense couldn't tell whether or not he was joking. Fergus, too, looked very grave.

"Still," said Fergus, "she's a pretty small girl to carry a sofa from the parlor to the barn and put a pig inside and sew him up."

"That's true," said Grandfather, nodding gravely. "We'll have to think of some one else. Perhaps it's Uncle Jonah," he added as Uncle Jonah at that moment came slowly around the corner of the barn.

Uncle Jonah also seemed to have something on his mind.

"Dem hosses," he began, "is sho' hoodooed."

"Have they been out again?" Grandfather demanded sharply.

"Yas suh, dey looks like it. But dat ain' all. Dat knife--I sho' don' like de looks ob dat."

"What knife are you talking about?" said Grandfather.

Without a word, Uncle Jonah led the way into the barn and pointed to Malay Kris. With some difficulty, Grandfather and Fergus pulled Kris free.

"It's beyond me," Grandfather said bewildered.

Fergus removed his hat and ran his fingers thoughtfully through his hair. Uncle Jonah shook his head and went away, muttering to himself.

Grandfather looked at Hortense with his sharp bright eyes, but she did not know how to begin an explanation, so complicated had matters become.

"Let's go in for breakfast, Hortense," Grandfather suggested.

CHAPTER XI

"... take us to the rock on the mountain side where the Little People dance."

That afternoon Andy and Hortense sat in the orchard eating apples.

"Do you suppose we'd grow little if we ate thirteen apples?" Hortense asked.

Andy, who had eaten six and lost his appetite, was of the opinion that they would grow bigger, could they eat so many. "Or maybe we'd burst," he added.

"We mustn't eat any more apples now," said Hortense, also finishing her sixth, "and don't eat too much supper."

"Why?" said Andy, unwilling to sacrifice his supper without a good reason.

"I've a plan," said Hortense. "We've got to eat thirteen cookies again and grow little--but I won't tell you what we'll do then, for it's to be a surprise!"

"We'll go through the little door again and find the Cat's house," Andy guessed.

"We must take Highboy and Lowboy for company," said she, "but Alligator and the others won't do at all. How much is four times thirteen?"

"Fifty-two," said Andy after a moment.

"That's a great many cookies," said Hortense. "I do hope Aunt Esmerelda bakes this afternoon so there are sure to be enough. You see, both Highboy and Lowboy will have to eat thirteen cookies, too, making fifty-two for all of us."

"I wonder how many Alligator would have to eat?" said Andy. "Most likely a whole jar full, he's so big."

"He can't ride anyhow," Hortense began, and then clapped her hand to her mouth and refused to say another word.

On her way to supper, however, she looked into the cooky jar and found it full to the top. She very carefully counted out fifty-two cookies and carried them up to her room in her apron.

That night, when all was still and Andy had come by his usual route through the basement, Hortense took him and Lowboy to her room.

"What's up to-night?" asked Lowboy. "Oh, I see, upstairs."

"If you make bad jokes, you can't come with us," Hortense warned him.

Lowboy promised to be good, and Hortense brought out the cookies and divided them into four piles of thirteen each.

"I know," said Lowboy, "we'll pretend that this is a midnight spread in boarding school. Jeremiah and Grater will be teachers who try to catch us and----"

"All you have to do is to eat your thirteen cookies," said Hortense, "all but a little piece of the last one which you must save and put in your pocket."

"After twelve to begin with, I can do that," joked Lowboy.

"If it kills me," said Highboy, "tell them I died a pleasant death."

Then nobody said a word for a while, and all ate their cookies. At the tenth, Highboy remarked that thirteen would be all he would want.

"I'll break my top off or lose a handle," said he, "but it's a nice game."

"What's happening to me?" asked Lowboy, after taking a bite of his thirteenth.

"Don't eat any more," Hortense warned him.

"How could I?" asked Lowboy. "I'm not a storeroom or a wardrobe trunk! Besides, your Grandmother has me half filled with her knitting and things. I must say I prefer cookies."

"I wish," said Highboy to Hortense, "that you hadn't packed away that last dress in my bottom drawer."

"Don't you see that you've grown small?" Hortense asked.

"Too small for the cookies," said Lowboy. "My clothes are so tight that I can't squeeze this last piece into my pocket."

"Now we're ready for the next part of the game," said Hortense, getting up.

"No running or anything like that," said Lowboy. "I can't do it."

"You'll only have to walk a short way, and after that it will be easy."

But Hortense had forgotten that to people as small as they had become, it was a long walk down the hall, and the stairs, and through the house.

"We should have eaten the cookies outside, of course," said she. "I didn't think."

However, following Hortense as leader, they finally reached the barn. Hortense stopped at the door.

"How will we ever get onto their backs?" said she. "Of course, we should have climbed on first and then eaten the cookies. I'm managing this very badly. Perhaps," she added hopefully, "they'll be lying down."

As luck would have it, Tom and Jerry were lying down in their stalls, for they were still weary from their adventure of the night before. Small as they were, Hortense and Highboy had no great difficulty in scrambling up Tom's side and taking a firm hold of his mane, nor did Jerry object when Andy and Lowboy mounted him. Tom looked at his riders in mild surprise, but made no move to get up.

"What next?" asked Lowboy.

"You'll see," said Hortense, who began to repeat the charm which Grater had spoken:

> Ride, ride, ride
> For the world is fair and wide.
> The moon shines bright
> On a magic night,
> And Tom and Jerry
> Are able very
> To ride, ride, ride.

At the first words Tom turned reproachful eyes upon her.

"I didn't think it of you, Hortense," said he. "Jerry and I are worn out with riding, and here you abuse us, too."

"We'll be easy on you," said Hortense. "You have only to take us to the rock on the mountain side where the Little People dance. There you may rest until we return home. Besides, if we left you here Grater and Jeremiah might come and ride again."

"That is true," said Tom, "and another such ride as last night's would be the end of me."

"Quick then, to the rock," said Hortense, and in a twinkling Tom and Jerry were out of the barn and soaring high in the air over the field and the orchard, over the brook and the tree tops beyond. The moon shone full and bright upon them, and every one was so thrilled with its brightness that he felt like singing. Lowboy did break into a song, but Hortense silenced him at once for fear of frightening the Little People.

Over the tree tops they came and down towards the rock. Hortense could see the Little People dancing, but before Tom and Jerry could alight, the Little People had seen them and disappeared into the mountain.

"After them, quick," Hortense cried, slipping from Tom's back, and the others followed her as she ran into the entrance to the mountain.

The passage was small and dark and wound this way and that. Soon it ended, and Hortense and the others came into the land where the blue moon was shining as before. But nowhere was there any sign of the Little People.

"What shall we do now?" Hortense asked when they had all stopped, not knowing what to do next.

"It's your party," said Lowboy. "You say what we shall do."

"There's a path," said Andy, pointing to a way among the trees.

"I believe," said Highboy, who had been looking around, "that these are raspberries on this bush. Um--um--good," and he began to eat as rapidly as he could pick them.

With difficulty Lowboy dragged his brother away from the tempting fruit and after Andy and Hortense, who had gone down the path. The path wandered every which way and seemed to go on forever.

"This isn't the way to the Cat's house at any rate," said Hortense, stopping to take breath, for they had gone at a rapid pace.

"What's that?" exclaimed Highboy.

All listened intently. There seemed, indeed, to be something moving among the bushes. Almost as soon as it started, the slight noise stopped, and they went on.

The path suddenly came to an end in an open place. Hortense and the others paused to look around, and as if by magic, innumerable Little People appeared on all sides--archers in green coats, armed with bows and arrows; pike-men in helmets and breastplates, and swordsmen with great two handled swords slung across their backs.

The captain of the fairy army, a fierce little man with a pointed mustache, stepped forward.

"Yield!" he commanded in a sharp voice. "You are prisoners! Bind them and take them to the King."

His men did as they were bid, and in a twinkling Hortense and Andy and Highboy and Lowboy found themselves with bound hands, marching forward, surrounded by the armed Little People.

"We are bound to have a trying time," said Lowboy, joking as usual. "The King will try us."

Hortense and Andy were too depressed to enjoy jokes, and Highboy, with tears streaming down his cheeks, was composing a poem bidding a sad farewell to home and friends. Hortense could hear him trying rhymes to find one which would fit--"home, moan, bone, lone."

"Those don't rhyme," said Hortense irritably. "It must end with *n*, not *n*."

"But so few good words end in *m*," Highboy protested. "There's *roam* of course. That might do. For instance,

If once again I see my home Never more at night I'll roam.

Not bad is it?"

Hortense thought it very bad indeed but didn't say so, for Highboy was finding pleasure in his rhymes and she hadn't the heart to depress him. She held tight to Andy's hand and walked on without speaking.

They were marched into a little glade, brightly lighted with glowworms and fireflies imprisoned in crystal lamps. The Queen sat upon her throne, but the King walked up and down in front of his and tugged at his tawny beard, and he looked very fierce.

"Here are the prisoners, your Majesty," said the captain of the guard, saluting.

"Ha," said the King. "Good, we'll try and condemn them at once."

"Please, your Majesty," said Hortense timidly, "we've done nothing wrong."

"I'll be the judge of that," said the King. "Prisoners are always guilty. However, you'll have a fair trial; I'll be the judge myself. What have you to say for yourselves?"

"We were seeking your assistance against Grater," said Hortense. "That is why we came to you."

The King shuddered, and all the Little People standing near by turned pale.

"He is never to be mentioned in my presence," said the King. "The penalty is ten years' imprisonment. Besides, how can you know so much about--him--unless you are his servants? It stands to reason that you are not telling the truth."

"Oh dear!" said Hortense. "How unfair you are!"

"It's a first principle of law that what a prisoner says is untrue," said the King. "I always go on that principle, and that is why I am always right."

"And you'd rather be right than be King, of course," said Lowboy.

"Silence!" roared the King. "Who dares speak so to me?"

The guard thrust Lowboy forward so that the King could see him better.

"A low fellow," said the King.

"But always in high spirits," said Lowboy.

"I am the only one here who is allowed to make jokes," said the King.

"It must be great to be a king," said Lowboy.

"It is," said the King. "Take this fellow and set him to weeding the royal strawberry beds for ten years. And you," he said, turning to Highboy, "stole my raspberries. Since you like them so well, you may pick them for ten years. Away with them! As for you two," pointing to Andy and Hortense--

Here the Queen interrupted.

"They look like a nice little boy and girl," said she. "Keep them until morning and then look further into the matter. Perhaps they are speaking the truth. I'm sure they are." And she smiled upon them.

The King walked up and down for a moment, without speaking.

"Very well. Be it as you wish," he agreed at last. "It is the Queen's privilege to command clemency."

"She should have some privilege if she has to laugh at the royal jokes," said Lowboy.

"Fifteen years!" roared the King. "I told you to put that fellow to work."

The guards hurried Lowboy and Highboy away, and Andy and Hortense were left alone.

"These two may be imprisoned in the pine tree," said the King, "until morning. Then I'll decide what further to do with them."

Six of the little soldiers took Andy and Hortense by the arm and led them to the foot of a big pine tree. Taking a key from his pocket, the officer in command unlocked a little door in the trunk of the tree, Hortense and Andy entered their prison, and he closed and locked the door after them. It was very dark, but as their eyes became accustomed to it, Andy and Hortense could see a little.

The hollow trunk made a round room, which was carpeted with pine needles for a bed. There was nothing else whatsoever. Above them the room reached high into the trunk, and at the very top they could see a little patch of light.

"It's probably a knot hole," said Andy, "and if we could climb so high, we might crawl through and get outside."

"We couldn't get down without being seen even then," reasoned Hortense.

"There's a chance," said Andy. "Anyway, they might not see us and just decide we had already escaped. It's worth trying."

"Very carefully they searched the trunk of the tree, seeking something that would help them climb.

"Here's something that looks like a crack in the trunk," said Andy. "If I could get a foothold in that, I believe I could climb to the top. Give me a hand here."

Hortense did as she was bid, and Andy began to climb.

"It gets easier," he said in a moment. "Can you find a foothold and follow me?"

Try as she would, Hortense couldn't manage a start.

"I'll come back," said Andy, descending until he could give Hortense a hand. With Andy's aid Hortense succeeded in climbing a few feet and after that was able to make her own way.

Up and up they climbed, coming at last to the hole at the top which was just big enough to crawl through. Outside was a great limb, and on this they rested.

"The Little People will hardly see us here, we're so high up," said Andy.

"But we can't get down," said Hortense, "so it does us little good."

Andy made no reply, for he was looking about him.

"These trees grow very close together," said he. "I believe I'll see where this branch goes."

Off he went, and Hortense waited. At last he came back, saying, "We can get to the next tree, and from that to another. When we are far enough away from the sentry, we'll try to climb down."

With Andy leading the way, they went out to the end of the branch which just touched the branch of the next tree. Onto this they were able to climb, and they made their way slowly to the trunk; then out on a branch on the other side, and so to the next tree. In this way they progressed from tree to tree, but each was as big as the last and it was impossible for such little people as they to climb down.

"We might eat a bite of cooky and grow big," said Hortense.

"Then we couldn't get out of the tunnel," said Andy, "and we'd have to stay here forever."

They seemed to be in a bad fix, indeed.

"If we could only fly," said Hortense, "how nice it would be."

"That's an idea," said Andy.

Looking about him a moment, he began to climb to the branch above.

"Come here," he called, and Hortense followed.

At the base of the branch there was a hole in the tree, and, looking through this, they saw a snug nest lined with twigs and moss.

"It's the nest of some big bird," said Andy. "We'll wait here and ask him to take us down."

It seemed the only thing to do and, making themselves as comfortable as they could, they set themselves to wait.

The blue moon rose higher and higher, and they became quite stiff.

"It may be a last year's nest," said Hortense.

"Or an owl's, and he won't come home until morning," said Andy.

They had almost fallen asleep when something big and white sailed down and alighted on the branch--a great owl like the one on Grandmother's mantel, with fierce, bright eyes.

"Who, who are you?" said the Owl. "And what are you doing at my door?"

"Please, sir," said Hortense, "we want to get down to the ground and cannot."

"Fly down," said the Owl.

"We can't fly," said Hortense.

"How absurd," said the Owl. "You shouldn't climb trees then."

"We had to, to get away from the Little People," helped Andy.

"So that's it," said the Owl. "They are a nuisance, I'll admit, spoiling all the hunting with their songs and dancing. I'm inclined to help you. What will you give me if I carry you down?"

Andy and Hortense searched their pockets and turned out a piece of string, a top, five jacks, a pocketknife, and two not very clean handkerchiefs.

"Those are of no use to me," said the Owl.

"We have nothing else except some pieces of cooky," bargained Hortense.

"Very well," the Owl grumbled, "I'll take them--though it's not enough."

Hortense gave him her cooky--all but a tiny piece which she saved to eat when she wanted to grow big again. The Owl swallowed it in one gulp.

"Very good cooky," he commented, "though I should prefer a little more molasses. Get on my back."

Hortense obeyed, and the Owl spread his great wings. Out and out he soared and then came gently to earth, and Hortense slipped off his back.

"Thanks very much," said she.

"Don't mention it," said the Owl and, spreading his wings, soared away into the tree.

A moment later Andy was beside her.

"If you cross the strawberry field and the raspberry patch," the Owl suggested, "you'll come to a path that goes by the house. If you can get by that unseen, perhaps you can escape."

"What house?" Hortense asked.

The Owl ruffled out his feathers fiercely.

"The house where that miserable Cat lives with the bright thing," said he.

The Owl flew away and Andy and Hortense started to run across the strawberry field, stopping now and then to eat the ripe, sweet berries. In the middle of the field they noticed something black. Its presence frightened them, and they feared to go close to it. However, it did not move for some moments, and cautiously they drew nearer. It was Lowboy, fast asleep.

Hortense shook him and he opened his eyes.

"Get up and come home," said Hortense. But Lowboy would not move.

"I've eaten so many strawberries that I can't budge," said he.

"Then we'll have to leave you," Hortense replied.

"There are worse fates than fifteen years of such strawberries," said Lowboy. "Perhaps, though, I'll get away sometime and find the road home."

"Where's Highboy?" Hortense demanded.

"Over there in the raspberry patch," said Lowboy, "but I fear he's in as bad shape as I am."

And so it proved, for when they came upon Highboy in the middle of the patch he was seated on the ground, lazily picking berries from the stems about his head.

"Get up and come with us," Hortense commanded.

Highboy shook his head.

"I must serve my sentence," said he. "After that, if I'm not turned into a raspberry tart, I'll try to find my way home. The only thing is that I find it hard to write poetry when I've eaten so much. Poetry should be written on an empty stomach. I can't think of a rhyme for raspberry."

"I don't believe there is one," said Hortense. "What difference does it make, anyhow?"

"Ah," said Highboy, "you're not a poet and don't know what it is to want a rhyme."

So Andy and Hortense sadly left him and by and by came to the other side of the raspberry patch and to the path of which the Owl had spoken.

"I suppose we must try to reach home this way," said Hortense, "for we daren't go by the Little People again."

"One way is about as bad as another," Andy agreed.

"If we meet Jeremiah and Grater, we'll eat our cooky quick," Hortense said. "Then they won't be so formidable."

"And then we'd never get through the tunnel," finished Andy.

However, they kept on along the path which they had traveled before and after a while came to the little gate beyond which lay the Cat's house. There was no light except the gleam of the fire upon the windowpane.

Andy and Hortense hesitated.

"Let's look in," said Andy. "Perhaps no one's at home."

"And then I might find my charm," Hortense added eagerly.

They peeped through the window and saw nothing but a low fire on the hearth and the dim, kindly face of the big clock.

"Let's risk it," said Hortense and lifting the latch, walked in.

"Hello," said the Clock genially. "You here again? It's a dangerous place for little folks."

"We shan't stay," said Hortense. "I want to get my charm if I can."

But the charm was not in its place under the glass upon the mantel.

"Oh dear," said Hortense.

"Jeremiah took the charm away," said the Clock. "Perhaps he'll bring it back in time."

"You have all the time there is," Hortense said. "We haven't and can't wait so long."

Still, there was nothing to do, not then at least, and bidding the Clock good-by, she and Andy hurried away. The blue moon was setting, and soon, they knew, it would be day. They hastened their steps and had nearly reached the tunnel when Andy suddenly pulled Hortense into the bushes beside the path.

Down the path came the sound of footsteps and past them hurried Jeremiah and Grater.

"Let's hurry," said Andy, "before they come back."

They ran down the tunnel as fast as they could and soon came to the large cave under the brook where the water dripped without ceasing.

"Safe so far," said Andy, "but the last part is uphill and harder."

They crossed the cave and ran on, looking back now and then as they paused to catch their breath.

"We're lucky," said Andy when they had passed the little door safely and shut it behind them.

They slipped through the wooden chute into the cellar and seated themselves on the stairs to eat their bites of cooky.

"Oh," said Hortense suddenly, "what do you suppose will become of Tom and Jerry? I'd forgotten them completely."

"We'll have to wait and see," said Andy. "I'm sleepy and must get to bed."

So, too, was Hortense, and she did not awaken in the morning until ten o'clock when the sun was shining high. Her only thought was of Tom and Jerry and what might have become of them, until she tried to open a drawer in the highboy to find a dress when she also remembered that Highboy and Lowboy were imprisoned.

The drawer wouldn't open; it was stuck fast. So, too, were the other drawers. Nor when she spoke to Highboy did he answer; he was not there. Only a dead thing of wood stood where Highboy had been.

"Dear me," thought Hortense, "I suppose it is the same with Lowboy. How then, will Grandmother get at her knitting?"

She hastily dressed in the clothes she had worn the day before. Breakfast was over, and Hortense begged Aunt Esmerelda for a bite in the kitchen. Aunt Esmerelda was muttering to herself.

"Dis yere house is sho' hoodooed. Mah cookies is gone, an' I done made a crock full yistahday. An' yo' gran'ma's chist of drawahs, dey don' open. An' de hosses is plumb gone. It ain't no place fo' me."

Hortense kept a discreet silence and hurriedly finished her breakfast. Then she ran to her Grandmother.

"I shall have to get Fergus to pry open the drawer of the lowboy," said Grandmother. "It won't open at all." Then noticing Hortense's soiled dress for the first time, she added,

"Dear me, child, you should have on a clean dress."

"The drawer in the highboy wouldn't open, Grandma," said Hortense.

"And your Grandfather is looking for the horses. They have disappeared," said Grandmother. "I'm sure I don't know what is the matter with everything."

Hortense ran out to the barn to find her Grandfather. Fergus, Uncle Jonah, and Grandfather were standing before the barn discussing the loss of Tom and Jerry. Hortense stood quietly by, listening to what they said, but all the time her eyes were on the mountain side, seeking the rock where last evening she had left Tom and Jerry. She found it at last and watching it closely, saw something move.

"I think Tom and Jerry are way up on the mountain side by that big rock," said she pointing.

Grandfather and Uncle Jonah could see nothing, but Fergus, whose eyes were good, said finally, "I see something moving there, to be sure, but how Tom and Jerry could reach such a place, I can't see. However, I'll go look."

Uncle Jonah shook his head and went away muttering; Hortense, holding her Grandfather's hand, went with him to his library. Grandfather took her on his knee and for a while said nothing--just sat with wrinkled brows, thinking. Then he raised his eyes to the bronze Buddha and spoke, half to himself.

"I believe if we could make the image talk we'd learn what's at the bottom of all these mysterious happenings. He looks as if he could talk, doesn't he? Perhaps if we burned incense before him he might speak."

"What is incense?" Hortense asked.

"This," said Grandfather, opening a drawer and showing her a sweet-smelling powder. "If we burned this before him and he were pleased with us, he might be made to talk. So the Hindoos believe. But I'm afraid he'd pay no attention to unbe-lievers."

Grandfather was joking, of course, but nevertheless Hortense pondered his words and made note of the drawer in which her Grandfather kept the little packet of incense.

Late that afternoon Fergus arrived home with Tom and Jerry, having had an awfully hard time getting them safely down the mountain side. It was so late that Fergus had no time to see to the drawers which refused to open in the lowboy and the highboy. For this Hortense was glad; she feared that it would hurt Highboy and Lowboy to have the drawers forced open and, besides, she meant that night to do her best to rescue them from the Little People. To that end she ran to the hedge which divided her yard from Andy's and, calling to Andy, told him her purpose.

CHAPTER XII

"There are queer doings in this house."

I think," said Hortense, "that every one should go with us to-night, Coal, Ember, Malay Kris, Owl, and even Alligator. For you see, not only do we have to free Highboy and Lowboy from the Little People, but we have to bring them safely home."

Andy thought for a moment.

"It will take a great many cookies," said he, "and it will probably be difficult to make Malay Kris, Owl, and Coal and Ember eat thirteen cookies each. Alligator, of course, will eat anything."

Hortense nodded.

"I've thought of that. I don't think Coal and Ember need be smaller than they are to get through the tunnel; nor Owl either. Malay Kris, I'm sure, will do as we ask him. That will make only four of us again, and fifty-two cookies as before. I do hope there are that many. Aunt Esmerelda says she's going to stop baking cookies, they go so fast."

Happily, the cooky jar was full again, and Hortense and Andy filled their pockets with the fifty-two cookies.

When it was dark and still, Hortense explained the plan to her companions. Alligator did not like the idea of becoming smaller, but the thought of the cookies, nevertheless, decided him. He ate them one after another as fast as Hortense could toss them into his mouth and at the thirteenth he became no larger than a little baby alligator. Malay Kris likewise ate his bravely and became small accordingly.

"Luckily, I'll be even sharper than before," said he.

Owl glared upon these proceedings with contempt.

"This is all foolishness," said he.

"But you'll come, won't you?" Hortense asked anxiously. "You can help us a great deal because you can see in the dark. Besides," she added, "we want your advice."

"Much heed you'll take of it," Owl grumbled. He was pleased, nevertheless, and swelled out his feathers complacently.

"Then let us start at once," said Hortense, leading the way.

She and Andy had decided that the tunnel way was best, for they could not easily climb the mountain and to ride on Tom and Jerry was to invite capture by the Little People, whom they must avoid.

They hurried as fast as they could and met no one. Their only difficulty was in getting Alligator through the cave under the brook, for he liked the feel of the water dripping on his hide. However, now that he was small he was easier to manage than before, and Coal and Ember dragged him away despite his protests.

When at last they came out from the tunnel, the blue moon was shining as before upon the roof of the Cat's house. The house itself was dark, but for a flicker of firelight on a windowpane.

"Look in and see if any one is there," Hortense whispered to Owl.

Obediently he flew and peered in at the window, returning to say that all he could see was the clock. So Hortense ventured in, finding the house empty as Owl had said, save for Grandfather's Clock.

"They're all out, tick tock," said the Clock. "But it is dangerous to remain, for Grater is very angry and desperate to-night."

Hortense looked in the glass case for her charm but could not find it.

"You had best get it back somehow," said the Clock. "It gives Jeremiah and Grater power."

"But how can I?" said Hortense anxiously.

"Who can say?" said the Clock. "But in time anything may happen."

"Do you know what will happen?" Hortense asked exasperatedly. "If you are Time, everything will happen in you, and so you must know what everything is and will be."

"I know, but I do not say," the Clock replied. "That is how I keep my reputation for wisdom."

Hortense hurried back to the others, and they proceeded beyond the house and through the woods until they neared the raspberry patch.

"You go ahead," said Hortense to Owl, "and spy out the land. Perhaps some of the Little People are about."

Owl flew off as directed and returned shortly to say, "Two of the guard are seated on the edge of the strawberry field. I could not hear what they said, but perhaps if you creep quietly through the bushes you can overhear."

Andy and Hortense, telling the others to wait, did as suggested. Creeping cautiously through the bushes, they could hear the little soldiers talking together before they could see them. Unfortunately, Andy stepped on a dry stem which broke with a snap. The soldiers ceased talking at once and Andy and Hortense lay still, scarcely daring to breathe.

"What was that?" asked one of the soldiers at last in a low voice.

"It must have been a bird," said the other. "I saw a great owl only a moment ago."

Then they resumed their talk.

"Well, it makes our work easier to have them gone," said one. "The short fat fellow was always eating the strawberries instead of putting them in his basket, and the tall one wouldn't work when he had a rhyme to find."

"And now," said the other, "they are to wear fine clothes and have nothing to do. It must have been the Queen who interceded for them."

"I don't call it nothing to do to make jokes all day or to write a poem when ordered," said the first.

"True," his companion replied. "I should rather pick berries. Meanwhile I'm going to take a nap. The Captain won't be back for hours."

"Me, too," the other agreed. "We'll lay our breastplates and helmets to hand and slip them on when we hear him coming."

Thereupon silence ensued, and Hortense and Andy lay still. It was evident, Hortense was thinking, that Highboy and Lowboy had been ordered back to court, and to help them escape would be difficult, for how dared she and Andy go near it, escaped prisoners as they were?

After a time Hortense nudged Andy and they crept forward together until, by parting the bushes, they could see the little soldiers fast asleep, their swords and armor beside them. Cautiously, Hortense reached out and drew a breastplate towards her and followed it by seizing a helmet and a sword. Andy, at a nod, did likewise, and with their captured arms they made their way slowly back through the bushes to a safe distance.

"We must put them on and disguise ourselves so that we can go to the court," said Hortense, slipping on the breastplate and helmet and buckling the sword-belt about her. "If we pull the visors of our helmets down, no one will recognize us."

"But what of the others?" Andy inquired, adjusting his armor.

Hortense clapped her hands.

"I know," said she, "we'll pretend we've captured them, and take them to the King."

"It will be all the harder for us to escape later," warned Andy.

"We must risk that," Hortense replied. "Besides, the Queen may aid us if we tell her everything. She is much kinder and wiser than the King."

So it was decided to lay the plan before the others, which they did.

"I'm content," said Owl, "for no one can keep me captive if I wish to escape."

"And I," said Malay Kris, "am afraid of nothing."

"I'll swallow any one who interferes with me," said Alligator.

"They'll not hurt us," said Coal and Ember growling.

"Then, if we're all agreed, let's go to the King's court," said Hortense, and with her and Andy leading the way, off they went.

The court was assembled in a glade in the woods, all the Little People grouped about their King and Queen. When Andy and Hortense appeared with their odd captives, way was made for them, every one staring in surprise. Even the King was dumb with astonishment.

"What have we here, a traveling circus?" said he at last.

"Prisoners we captured near the Royal Raspberry Patch," said Andy in as martial a tone as he could muster.

"Where could they come from and what are they doing here?" the King demanded. "Speak," he commanded them.

Owl took it upon himself to answer.

"We were hunting the great Cat and Grater, who are our enemies."

"So the boy and girl said who escaped the other night, no one knows how. For all we know, you may be servants of the terrible Grater of whom my most valiant soldiers are afraid, and of the great Cat with the claws."

"Show us either of them and we'll prove our quality," Malay Kris boasted. "I have once before run Grater through and pinned him to the floor."

The King pulled at his beard.

"It is true that I have heard he now wears a piece of pink court-plaster."

"Give me arms and put me into your service," said Malay Kris, "and I will prove my mettle."

"You are indeed a likely looking soldier," said the King, regarding him with favor. "I'm inclined to try you. Give him," said he to the Captain of the Guard, "armor and a sword, and we'll see what he can do. As for these others, we'll put them in cages for the present and decide later what to do with them."

At these words Owl flew into the top of a tree and hooted.

"I do not like cages," said he. "I prefer a tree top."

And though the King tried soft words and made promises, the Owl refused to budge, looking down upon them all with great round eyes.

Coal and Ember growled and showed their teeth, and Alligator opened wide his great jaws and lashed about with his tail; but the little soldiers threw themselves valiantly upon them and bore them away as the King ordered.

"You two," said the King to Andy and Hortense, "have proved yourselves brave and are deserving of reward. We attach you to our person. You may stand guard in the palace."

The Queen, who had been looking hard at Hortense, spoke.

"May I not have them?" said she.

"Certainly, my love," the King replied graciously. "All that is mine is yours. Besides, you may need stout protection from our enemy. Already it has taken from us our Court Jester and Court Poet." The King walked nervously up and down. "Our magic power is of no avail," said he, "against such evil."

Andy and Hortense, in obedience to the Queen's wish, took their place at the door of her apartment, and soon she called them to her.

"I see," said she to Hortense, "that you are the little girl who was here before, and this, I suppose, is the little boy. Now tell me all about it."

Hortense was much surprised but did as she was told, for she felt the Queen to be her friend.

"Alas," said the Queen, "Grater has already made prisoners of Highboy and Lowboy. I had persuaded the King to make them his Court Jester and Poet but before they could even be brought here, they were waylaid and borne away."

"In that case," said Hortense, "we must go to their rescue. Will you grant us permission?"

"Gladly," said the Queen, "although I cannot free the others without appealing to the King, and it is best for the present not to tell him who you are. I shall contrive to see Malay Kris and send him after you. Wait near by."

Accordingly, Andy and Hortense slipped out of the palace unseen and waited where they were joined shortly by Malay Kris, who was so eager for a fight that Andy and Hortense had to beg him to be cautious.

They quietly crept close to the Cat's house, and Owl, who had joined them, peeped in at the window.

"All quiet," said he.

The four entered.

"Highboy and Lowboy are in the cooky jar," said the Clock, not waiting to be asked. "Make haste!"

It was not easy to free them. The jar was far taller than Andy and Hortense, and as smooth and slippery as ice. Andy and Malay Kris finally made a rope by tying together table covers and sheets and, throwing the end of this over the edge of the jar, at last succeeded in pulling Highboy and Lowboy to the top. From this they dropped safely to the floor.

"Now we must hurry," said Hortense, and away they went.

But they were not in time, for barely had they reached the gate when they were seen by Jeremiah and Grater. Thereupon ensued a fierce battle. Jeremiah seemed as big as a lion. He lashed his bushy tail, arched his back, and spat; his great eyes glowed, and his claws were long and sharp as knives. Andy and Hortense were glad for their breastplates, for these the Cat's sharp claws could not pierce.

Highboy and Lowboy, however, had no armor.

"Oh, my nice coat of varnish!" Highboy moaned as Jeremiah's claws reached him.

"I shall no longer be a polished person," said Lowboy.

Hortense and Andy kept in front of the two in so far as they could, but with Jeremiah in front and Grater at one side they were hard-pressed.

"Get into the bushes," Andy ordered, and they retreated slowly into the raspberry patch.

Here Jeremiah was at a disadvantage, for the thorns tore his coat, and he could not use his claws freely. Thorns meant nothing to Grater, however, in his bright suit of mail. Malay Kris, undaunted, struck him a great blow and bore him to the ground.

"Tie his hands," cried Malay Kris.

Hortense and Andy, using their shoe laces for the purpose, bound Grater fast. Jeremiah, thereupon, yowled dismally and retreated towards the house.

"Let's hurry as fast as we can," Hortense ordered.

Malay Kris brought up the rear, prodding Grater to make him go faster; Owl flew ahead to spy out the way; and Andy and Hortense followed, running.

They reached the entrance of the tunnel and hurried in, expecting every moment to see Jeremiah reappear, and now, without the protection of the raspberry bushes, they feared his great claws. Safely they crossed the dripping cave and were halfway through the tunnel on the other side when they perceived Jeremiah hot after them.

"Grater!" shrieked Lowboy.

Grater had seized the moment while their backs were turned to free himself of the cords which bound him and was running rapidly up the tunnel.

"He'll close the door on us!" Malay Kris shouted, and set off in pursuit.

With dismay Hortense and Andy perceived that they must meet Jeremiah's attack, for Highboy and Lowboy were of no use in a fight. Here it was that Owl proved himself most unexpectedly useful. While Andy and Hortense backed slowly through the tunnel facing Jeremiah's claws, Owl tweaked his tail and pulled bits of fur from his back. Jeremiah's claws were useless against such a foe who flew away whenever Jeremiah turned on him.

So the retreat was effected in good order and without serious hurt to any one, while from the rear came the clash of arms and the shouts of Kris and Grater in fierce conflict. Kris, having eaten the thirteen cookies and reduced his size, found Grater a far more formidable foe than before. But though small, Kris was as fast as lightning and darted here and there, evading Grater's blows and putting in quick stabs. Although Grater came more and more to resemble a sieve, he still stood his ground with his back to the door, and until he was forced aside, escape was impossible.

Lowboy then displayed a courage and intelligence which his fondness for poor jokes led nobody to expect. Throwing himself at Grater's knees and holding them tight, he threw their enemy to the ground with a crash. Malay Kris quickly disarmed and bound him and the way was clear.

Jeremiah, seeing that the battle was won, turned tail and fled, Owl hooting derisively after him. Every one sat down to get his breath. Except for a few scratches no one suffered any mishap.

"We've finished them this time," Malay Kris said complacently. "We must put this fellow where he can do no more harm."

Grater glared at them.

"I'll get even with you!" he promised.

"You'll be old and rusted to pieces by the time you escape," Kris retorted and wedged him tight against the door so that it could not be opened nor could Grater stir a hand or foot.

"You'll have a nice rest here," said Malay Kris. "It is quiet and nobody will disturb you."

Thus they left Grater, grinding his teeth in rage, and made their way into the cellar.

While they were eating their bits of cooky to make them large again, Hortense said,

"How can we prevent Jeremiah from setting Grater free?"

"We must block the way on this side, too," said Andy, immediately rolling a barrel before the sliding door in the air chute of the furnace. Upon this he piled a heavy box.

"If Jeremiah can move those, he is a smart cat," said Andy.

"Jeremiah is a smart cat," Hortense said, "but it's the best we can do."

In the kitchen they parted company, and as soon as Hortense was in bed she fell fast asleep and did not wake until the sun was high the next day.

After breakfast Fergus came to pry open the drawers in the lowboy that had refused to budge the day before.

"There's nothing the matter with them," said Fergus as they slid open at a touch. "They are just as usual."

"Why, so they are," said Grandmother and opened the upper drawer. "What in the world is this?"

The drawer was filled tight full of strawberries packed in neat boxes--and on top lay thirteen cookies!

Grandmother looked on these with astonishment.

"Wild strawberries!" said she tasting one. "And at this time of the year, too. They are delicious."

Grandfather and Fergus looked astonished, and Fergus scratched his head.

"Well," said Grandfather, "let's look at the highboy in Hortense's room. There's no telling what we'll find there."

They went to Hortense's room and again Fergus pulled open the drawers without difficulty. Boxes and boxes of raspberries lay on top of Hortense's things--and again there were thirteen cookies!

Grandfather and Grandmother raised their hands in amazement. They found no words to express their wonder. Later, when Mary came to Grandmother and reported that the sofa in the parlor had disappeared, Grandmother simply said, "The firedogs are gone from the hearth, too. There are queer doings in this house."

Hortense spent the afternoon in the library with Grandfather, her chin on her hand, thinking. From time to time she glanced at the image of Buddha. She thought she might tell Grandfather about all the strange things that had happened to her, but before doing so she resolved to try a plan which his words had put into her head.

Now and then Grandfather looked at her curiously, but he asked no questions, and Hortense could not guess his thoughts.

CHAPTER XIII

"This is what was inside,"--

The little box of incense lay at the back of the drawer where Hortense had expected to find it. She laid it on top of Grandfather's desk.

It was really necessary to have a light in order to see what she was about, but a lamp or candle, either one, seemed out of place. There should be only enough light to see the expression on the face of the image. In a half-darkness, she thought, he would be more likely to speak.

She raised the window shades and threw the shutters open. Moonlight filled the room dimly and fell upon the bronze image, sitting as expressionless as ever, immovable. Hortense's heart failed her. Nothing, she felt, would ever bring words to the closed lips or a flutter to the heavy eyelids. However, there was nothing to do but try.

She poured a little of the incense on an ash tray and touched a match to it. The wisp of smoke, pallid in the moonlight, curled slowly upwards and was lost to sight. A strong sweet odor filled the room.

Hortense moved the tray to the edge of the desk directly in front of the image and sat down in her Grandfather's chair to wait, her eyes fixed upon the calm round face before her. It looked like the face of a woman she thought, not that of a man.

She could see not the slightest change in the image after ever so long a time, though her eyes never left it. The incense was slowly consumed, and Hortense arose and added more. Still she watched, endlessly it seemed, until finally her eyes closed and she must have slept for a little, for when she opened them again the moonlight was far brighter than before and the image stood out in the fanciful shadows.

Yes, surely, the hand that now lay open had been raised and closed before. And the eyes looked at her instead of over her! Her heart beat quicker.

"You have moved," she said without thinking.

There was a slight stir of the bronze lips; then a soft measured voice said, "I wait, what is it you ask?"

"I should like," Hortense said, "to get back my charm."

"Jeremiah has it," said the Image, "and Jeremiah is getting to be a nuisance. I shall have to cut his claws."

How the Image could cut Jeremiah's claws, Hortense didn't see.

"That is to say," the Image went on, "he needs to be taken down."

Down to what, Hortense wondered. She sat a long while waiting for the Image to say more, but apparently it had gone back to sleep.

"Dear me, how slow it is!" Hortense said to herself. "I suppose it's like Grandfather's Clock and has all the time in the world."

She sat very silent and once or twice almost fell asleep.

The moonlight continued its slow and silent way across the floor until at last it rested full upon the Image.

"If you will take a paper knife," said the Image as though it had ceased speaking but a moment before, "and trace the flower pattern on my back, beginning in the center, you will find something."

Hortense, wondering, did as she was told. On the back of the Image, as it had said, was the pattern of a flower. Hortense followed the curves of its petals with the point of the knife. Then to her surprise the flower swung inward on an invisible hinge and there before her was an opening just large enough for her hand. Her fingers closed on something round and hard like a marble, which in the moonlight shone with little bright flashes and crinkles of gold and blue and rose. Hortense knew it was some precious stone.

As she sat with it in her hand, she heard the soft patter of feet along the hall, and in a moment two great green eyes shone in the doorway. Hortense sat very still with the jewel sparkling in her hand. Jeremiah came forward a step or two, and then suddenly he spat so loudly that Hortense jumped.

With a howl Jeremiah turned and ran like one possessed. Hortense could hear his claws scratching on the stairs as he raced up and up, out of hearing. On the threshold of the door before her lay a small white object. Hortense stooped and picked it up. It was the monkey charm! She fastened it about her neck and turned to thank the Image. But the Image said never a word--just sat as motionless, staring into the distance, as though it had never spoken.

Hortense went to bed with the jewel tightly clutched in her hand and fell fast asleep. In the morning she went down to breakfast in high spirits, hardly believing that what had happened was real. In her hand still was the wonderful jewel which shone and sparkled as though lit with a thousand colored fires. She kept it hidden in her lap while she ate, and when she had finished, she followed her Grandfather into the library.

"Some one has been burning incense," said Grandfather, looking at her.

Hortense nodded and played with the monkey charm about her neck.

"I did it," she said.

Thereupon she climbed on Grandfather's knee and told him the whole story from the beginning. Grandfather said never a word, but from time to time he looked at Hortense as though he couldn't believe what she said. When she spoke of the flower on the back of the image, he turned it around and traced the pattern with the point of the paper knife as Hortense had done. The little door opened as before. Grandfather looked in.

"This is what was inside," Hortense said and opened her hand in which was the jewel.

Grandfather took it and examined it gravely.

"Do you remember the story I told you about my friend who sought a rare jewel and who, when he died, sent me this image? This must be the jewel he found. It has lain here all these years. It is very strange that you should have found it as you did--your story is very strange. But for the jewel, and the disappearance of the sofa and the firedogs, I could scarcely believe it."

"If you'll come, I'll show you the little door and the tunnel," Hortense said.

"It would be too small for me to approach," Grandfather said, "and I am much too old to eat thirteen cookies."

"But," Hortense urged, "I want you to go with me to see the Little People. I must get Alligator and Coal and Ember back."

Grandfather shook his head.

"If you visit the Little People again, I fear it will have to be with your own friends. But wait a while. We've had enough surprising experiences for a time."

"It's really Jeremiah who is the cause of everything," Hortense said.

As she spoke Jeremiah walked in slowly, a very dejected cat.

"Come here, sir," Grandfather said sternly.

Jeremiah meowed plaintively and jumped on Grandfather's knee.

"I hear you've been up to tricks," Grandfather said.

Jeremiah hung his head and meowed again.

"I see you are sorry and will not do it again," Grandfather said. "If you do----" Grandfather opened his hand and showed the jewel.

In a flash Jeremiah was off Grandfather's knee and running down the hall. Grandfather laughed and held up his hand on which was a long red scratch.

"Oh!" Hortense cried, "the Image said he would cut Jeremiah's claws."

"That was a figure of speech, evidently," Grandfather said. "Whenever Jeremiah is bad, we'll show him the jewel. I'll keep it for you. It must be very valuable. Some day it will be yours."

But Hortense thought less of the jewel than of the monkey charm about her neck. Besides, there were Alligator and Coal and Ember, still captive among the Little People. She wished Grandfather hadn't asked her to keep away from the Little People for a while, though Alligator and Coal and Ember were decidedly able to care for themselves, and Grater was securely bound and unable to do further harm.

"But, of course," said Hortense, "I can talk to Owl, and Malay Kris, and to Highboy, and Lowboy, and we can lay our plans for the rescue."

CHAPTER XIV

Rescue From the Mountain Side

Hortense sat quietly in the corner of the kitchen on a stool watching Aunt Esmerelda at her work. Aunt Esmerelda was unhappy, and the more she tried to do her work the more she complained, and every once in a while she took a long look at Hortense, as if accusing her of her trouble. The trouble was that Aunt Esmerelda was trying to make cole slaw and she couldn't find her grater to shred the cabbage. So she was trying to cut it up with the large butcher knife.

"I 'clare," Aunt Esmerelda grumbled half to herself, but just loud enough so she knew Hortense would hear, "this yere house is sho' nuff voodood. First of all this ornery cat gets himself into some mighty peculiar fixes, inside the sofa and chimney and such likes, then the grater begins to get all full of knife holes and now I cain't even find it at all." Hortense squirmed uneasily and wished somebody could help Aunt Esmerelda get a new grater. But she couldn't tell the cook where the grater was, or how it got there, or poor old Aunt Esmerelda might leave and never come back, frightened as she was of spooks and similar things. But she didn't want a new grater, either, for fear it might also help the cat free the old grater, for then there would be three of them to contend with. So she said nothing but just kicked her feet a bit and stared at the floor.

Just then Mary came in, and she and Aunt Esmerelda began to talk.

Mary said, "You know, the firedogs are missing and Grandmother is very unhappy about it, because she can't have a fire-place fire on these chilly evenings. And when I went in the parlor to dust today, the sofa is gone, too. None of these things ever happened before Hortense came. I can imagine she might have taken the firedogs, though I can't imagine why. But she is too little to move that big divan."

By now Hortense felt very uneasy, knowing that both the cook and the maid were suspicious of her activities. She was wishing desperately that she wouldn't have to look at them, when luckily Grandfather came into the kitchen on his way to the barn and asked her if she would like to go look at the horses with him. So she gladly left the kitchen.

On their way to the barn she finally said, "Grandfather, is Grandmother awfully unhappy about the firedogs?" At this her Grandfather appeared surprised, but finally admitted to her that Grandmother surely did miss her fireplace fire in the evenings when she had tea.

"Well," said Hortense, "I've been trying to think of a plan to rescue the firedogs and the alligator sofa, but I need your help."

Grandfather took a long look at her, and Hortense was a little frightened that maybe she shouldn't have asked him at all. Finally he said, "I don't know how much help I could be. These magic things only happen to you because you are young and believe they can happen. But I am old, and need my sleep at night. However, maybe I could get Fergus to help you."

At the barn they found Fergus grooming Tom and Jerry. Uncle Jonas was there too, so until he left nothing more could be said about it, for he would have been frightened even worse than Mary or Aunt Esmerelda if he knew what was going on around the farm since Hortense's arrival. After an hour or so Grandfather sent Uncle Jonas to town for some harness straps and he and Hortense were free to talk to Fergus.

"Well, Hortense," began Grandfather, "why don't you tell Fergus about your adventures?"

Fergus looked strangely at the girl, but said nothing. Hortense hardly knew where to start, but finally began at the first and told him the whole story, just as she had Grandfather. When she finished Grandfather said, "Hortense says she has a plan for rescuing the firedogs and alligator sofa from the little people, but she needs some help. I wondered if you could help her, Fergus?"

Fergus thought this over for some time. Then he began to talk slowly, as if thinking aloud, and as if no one were hearing him at all. "It would be nice," he began, "if I didn't have to be grooming these horses so much. But if I were to go up there on the mountain side what could I tell Mary? I couldn't tell her the real story, because she'd never believe it. She might even get Aunt Esmerelda and Uncle Jonas all excited and there's no telling what would happen then. On the other hand I wouldn't want to tell her something that isn't true, either. But I sure would like to get this household back to normal again."

"Let me make a suggestion," offered Grandfather. "Why not tell her that I think somebody is bothering the horses at night and I want you to stay in the barn and guard them. If she is frightened to stay at your house alone all night I'm sure Grandmother would come stay with her for one night."

"That is so," said Fergus. "It is true that someone *has* been bothering the horses. Now I want to know what Hortense's plan is before I finally decide whether to risk my neck for those firedogs and that sofa."

"Well," Hortense began, "I thought if Andy and I were to go back to the little people by making ourselves small, then after we have had time to free the firedogs and alligator sofa, we'll wait there and you come get us by saying the magic words to Tom and Jerry. Then we can all ride the horses home."

"That sounds sensible," answered Fergus, "but how do you think you can free alligator sofa and Coal and Ember? And also what if Jeremiah should trap you in the tunnel?"

"Maybe I could keep the cat locked in the basement," suggested Grandfather. "That way I can help, too."

Hortense was much relieved to see that Grandfather and Fergus were willing to help her, and she surely felt much more secure with Jeremiah safely out of the way. As for getting Coal and Ember and alligator sofa, she thought the queen of the little people would help her if she explained how much it was troubling her Grandmother, and in fact upsetting the entire household.

So it was agreed. Just to be safe, Hortense planned to take Malay Kris along, since he had proved himself such a good fighter in other close scrapes. Now if only there would be the fifty-two cookies needed, thirteen apiece for Fergus, Malay Kris, Andy and herself.

When Hortense went back to the kitchen Aunt Esmerelda was dozing in the corner, her apron thrown up over her head. Hortense quietly sneaked over to the cookie jar and peeked in. The jar was full to the brim, so Hortense began busily putting cookies into her apron and dress pockets, counting carefully. Just as she was about done counting them out she felt a strange tickling on her leg. This so startled her that she knocked the lid to the cookie jar to the floor with a crash, and she saw Jeremiah disappear around the corner. The sudden noise woke Aunt Esmerelda, and the old cook opened her eyes wide when she saw Hortense with cookies bulging from every pocket.

"So tha's where all my cookies done go!" exclaimed the cook. "That yere girl is done takin' 'em by the dozen. Whoffo you wants all those cookies, girl? Doan you-all know you might git sick a-eatin' so much?"

Hortense had to do some very fast thinking, now, for she knew she didn't dare scare poor old Aunt Esmerelda by telling her the cookies were magic. So she said, "Please, Aunt Esmerelda, don't be angry. Your cookies are just so good I could eat them all day without getting sick. I was getting few more than usual just now because I was going to share them with some friends of mine. I really wouldn't try to eat these all by myself."

"Hermpf," snorted Aunt Esmerelda. "I suppose yo' friends include dat good for nuttin' Andy, whose all da time botherin' Uncle Jonas hawses. But dats all right, chile; ef you likes my cookies, you jus hep yoself to dem. Dat's what day is fo."

That evening, after supper when they were all having a cup of tea in the parlor Grandmother took a long look at Hortense, but said nothing. Grandfather took a few puffs on his pipe and Jeremiah walked in.

"That cat has just been in too much mischief lately," declared Grandfather. "I believe I'll try locking him the basement tonight and see if he will stay out of trouble." At this Jeremiah arched his back and started for the door, but Grandfather jumped up quickly and caught him.

"Don't blame the cat," Grandmother admonished. "After all you know very well there have been strange goings on which the cat certainly couldn't account for--like the disappearance of the sofa."

"Nevertheless, he's been in his share of trouble, what with jumping down the chimney and all," retorted Grandfather. "We'll try it for a night or two this way, anyway." So against the plaintive cries of the cat, the cellar door was locked securely after he was put downstairs.

Later, when everyone had retired, Hortense could hear Grandfather and Grandmother talking in their bedroom, but try as she could she couldn't catch a word they were saying, and she wondered if he might have told Grandmother about the plan to go to the little people again. However, after some time the conversation ceased and when all was quiet Hortense quietly slipped downstairs and told Malay Kris of the plan. He jumped down from the wall quickly.

"There's nothing I'd like better than a battle," he said. "Now that Grater is out of the way maybe I can get a taste of that cat. He'd be a nice juicy bite I fancy."

The two of them slipped out to the barn where they met Fergus and Andy.

"Now," said Hortense, dividing up the cookies, "Andy and Kris and I will go on the back to the attic and eat our cookies, then go through the tunnel to the place of the little people on the mountain side. The moon is just beginning to rise, so when it is directly overhead, Fergus can eat his cookies and fly to meet us with Tom and Jerry. That should give us time enough to rescue Coal and Ember and alligator sofa."

On arriving at the attic and dropping down into the secret room, they sat down and ate their cookies, then climbed on down the ladder to the secret passage to the tunnel. When they came to the door and opened it, imagine their surprise to find Grater untied and standing directly in their path. Before they could retreat, they heard soft padded feet and on turning around found Jeremiah staring intently at them, his eyes a brilliant green.

"Well, well, well," purred the cat. "This time it looks like our turn," and quick as a flash Jeremiah caught Hortense with one paw and Andy with the other, while Grater jumped on Malay Kris and they tied all three of them with the cords which had been holding Grater.

"You forgot," said Jeremiah, "that the trap door from the chute outside was open, so I got here ahead of you and untied Grater. Then we just decided to wait for you, figuring you'd be along."

Meanwhile Grater began to run his prickly sides on Malay Kris so he was no longer a sharp knife, just a dull old one. All the time Kris tried to wriggle free of his ties, but could not.

"Enough of this," said Jeremiah, "let's get rid of these pests once and for all. But first I believe I'll have the charm." So saying, he took the monkey charm from Hortense, who could do nothing to stop him. Then the cat and the grater marched their captives through the tunnel to their house.

"Before, when we put them in the cookie jar, they escaped," said Jeremiah.

"Why not lock them in the clock case," suggested Grater.

"Splendid idea," agreed Jeremiah, so they unlocked the door and pushed them all inside, carefully locking them in and Grater put the key in his pocket.

"Now," said Jeremiah, "let's go out on the mountain side and maybe we can catch a couple of those little people and really have a fine supper."

After they left Hortense began to cry softly. "Whatever will happen to us now," she sobbed, and sat down on one of the pendulum weights of the clock.

"If you don't get off my weights I'm afraid I'll have to stop," spoke up the clock. "And if time stands still then you certainly will never go anywhere."

"Oh, excuse me," said Hortense. "I quite forgot where we were." Then a sudden thought came to her. "Can you help us?" she asked.

"I'm afraid not," said the clock. "You see, time can't be on anybody's side, but must be on all sides."

"If you are on all sides, then you must be on our side," reasoned Hortense. "Anyway, do you know any way we can get out of your inside?"

While Hortense and the clock were thus talking, Malay Kris was rubbing his ropes against one of the weights, and finally succeeded in freeing himself. Then he quickly jumped up and untied Hortense and Andy, and then tried his point in the keyhole. By luck when the grater dulled his edges, he made them exactly fit the notches in the keyhole. "Now," he called, "if you can turn me over I believe I can turn the lock."

With Hortense standing on Andy's shoulders she could just reach Malay Kris, and with all her effort she turned the knife, the lock opened and the door swung out. Quickly the three friends left the cat's house and started through the garden toward the mountain side where the little people were.

As they came close to where the guards were, Andy sneezed. One of the guards saw them and raised the alarm and all the guards came running. Malay Kris tried defending them, but his edge was so dull that he could make no dent on their armor at all. So, once again, they were subdued, tied up, and brought before the king and queen.

"So," cried the king, "we have you again. This time we'll put you away for good.

But first search them. I don't want them to have any secrets hidden in their pockets." So the guards went through their pockets and found the pieces of cookie.

"They have no secret weapons, your honor," said the guards. "The only thing we found are these pieces of cookies."

"Bring me the cookies," ordered the king. "They should be a nice dessert for me." So saying he bit off a piece of one, and finding it very delicious, passed the others around to the rest of his guards. Hortense tried to stop him from eating any more, but as soon as she started to talk, he roared, "Silence from the prisoners! You will speak only if asked to." Then he distributed the remainder of the cookies among his guards until they were all eaten up. After having finished such a good dessert, he leaned back in this throne and, addressing himself to the three, said, "Have you any final words to say before I sentence you? Since you escaped once before, this time I intend to throw you in the dungeon beneath the mountain. No one has ever escaped from it."

Hortense and Andy were so frightened they couldn't say a word. But the queen came to their rescue. "Your honor," she said, "it is true that these strangers escaped once before. However, I can't see that they mean us any harm. Perhaps they could even be of some help to us if we kept them here."

"Ha!" cried the king. "Much help they'd be. They may even be spies from another land."

"From another land we are," spoke up Malay Kris. "And we do have some special news for you, if you care to know."

"How is that?" roared the king.

"First," said Malay Kris, "free Coal and Ember and Alligator sofa. We came here in order to free them."

"So they are your friends," said the King. "Well, you can have that alligator. His appetite is much too big for us. But the firedogs are serving the queen in her bedroom and she would have to free them if anyone does. In the meantime I'll think this over. Guards! Take them away!"

So the guards led Hortense, Andy, and Malay Kris away to a large open field where Alligator sofa lay sound asleep. A great number of guards were placed all around so there was no chance of escape.

"How will we ever get back home now," Hortense said softly to Andy. "The king ate all the rest of the cookies so we can't ever grow to our normal size again."

But Andy was looking up in the yellow sky. The dark blue moon had risen high overhead and the shadows of the dark red trees stood out like more sentries guarding the prisoners. As Andy watched he knew there wasn't a minute to spare, for soon Fergus would be coming on Tom and Jerry and if the little people were frightened back into the mountain and they were put in the dungeon beneath the mountain, that might be the end of the story. So he started up to one of the guards to demand to be taken to the king again. Before he had done two steps, however, Alligator sofa roused from his nap and said, "Did I hear someone say they wanted some cookies? I'm full of them. Just open my side a bit there, Malay Kris, and help yourself."

Kris quickly opened the sofa and all his cookies fell out on the ground. They quickly filled their pockets, just as the king came up to them.

"How is this? More cookies?" asked the king, surprised.

The queen had heard about the good cookies and came around, too, Coal and Ember on a leash. Just then they heard a soft pad-padding and creaky sounds as the cat and the grater suddenly appeared. At the same moment, the moon began to darken as the outline of Tom and Jerry appeared closer and closer.

"Run for your lives," screamed the king, and all the little people ran pell mell for the opening above the rock on the side of the mountain. Hortense, Andy and Malay Kris all took a bite of cookie and suddenly grew to their full size. Hortense seized Jeremiah and got her charm off his neck, but not before she got scratched deeply on the arm. Andy and Malay Kris dived for Grater, and he jumped backwards, right into the mouth of Alligator sofa.

When Fergus landed with Tom and Jerry, he also took the last bite of cookie and looked around. By this time the little people were all gone and Jeremiah had likewise disappeared. The moon was getting low in the sky, and so he gathered all the friends together.

"Soon it will be daylight," he said. "Until then, I think we'd better all stay together here, rather than risk getting lost trying to get down the mountain at night." So Hortense and Andy curled up on the sofa, Coal and Ember lay down beside Tom and Jerry, and Fergus sat up with Malay Kris to keep guard.

When the first red streaks of sunshine began to appear, all the magic had gone with the night. Coal, Ember and Malay Kris again became cold pieces of brass and steel, and the sofa looked just like any other piece of furniture. Fergus shook Andy and Hortense, and when they were awake he explained that they needed to get home by breakfast and it was a long climb down the mountain. So they tied the sofa on Tom's back, and Fergus helped Hortense and Andy on Jerry's broad back. He stuck Malay Kris in a loop of his belt, and picked up the firedogs. Slowly, this strange procession wound its way down the steep mountain, across the brook, and up through the apple orchard toward the big house. By the time they arrived at the barn, Grandfather was there to greet them.

"We're all back home, alive and well," he said. "I think we had better keep it this way." With a twinkle in his eye he continued. "There is a letter for Hortense in the morning mail. It says her folks are home from Australia, so she's to get on the train this afternoon and we'll not see her again until Christmas."

So this ends the strange adventure of Hortense and the cat in Grandfather's house. Nobody ever sat on the sofa again, however, for it felt lumpy.

The Codes Of Hammurabi And Moses
W. W. Davies

QTY

The discovery of the Hammurabi Code is one of the greatest achievements of archaeology, and is of paramount interest, not only to the student of the Bible, but also to all those interested in ancient history...

Religion   **ISBN:** *1-59462-338-4*   **Pages:132**
MSRP $12.95

The Theory of Moral Sentiments
Adam Smith

QTY

This work from 1749. contains original theories of conscience amd moral judgment and it is the foundation for systemof morals.

Philosophy   **ISBN:** *1-59462-777-0*   **Pages:536**
MSRP $19.95

Jessica's First Prayer
Hesba Stretton

QTY

In a screened and secluded corner of one of the many railway-bridges which span the streets of London there could be seen a few years ago, from five o'clock every morning until half past eight, a tidily set-out coffee-stall, consisting of a trestle and board, upon which stood two large tin cans, with a small fire of charcoal burning under each so as to keep the coffee boiling during the early hours of the morning when the work-people were thronging into the city on their way to their daily toil...

Childrens   **ISBN:** *1-59462-373-2*

Pages:84
MSRP $9.95

My Life and Work
Henry Ford

QTY

Henry Ford revolutionized the world with his implementation of mass production for the Model T automobile. Gain valuable business insight into his life and work with his own auto-biography... "We have only started on our development of our country we have not as yet, with all our talk of wonderful progress, done more than scratch the surface. The progress has been wonderful enough but..."

Biographies/   **ISBN:** *1-59462-198-5*

Pages:300
MSRP $21.95

The Art of Cross-Examination
Francis Wellman

QTY

I presume it is the experience of every author, after his first book is published upon an important subject, to be almost overwhelmed with a wealth of ideas and illustrations which could readily have been included in his book, and which to his own mind, at least, seem to make a second edition inevitable. Such certainly was the case with me; and when the first edition had reached its sixth impression in five months, I rejoiced to learn that it seemed to my publishers that the book had met with a sufficiently favorable reception to justify a second and considerably enlarged edition. ..

Pages:412

Reference ISBN: *1-59462-647-2*   *MSRP $19.95*

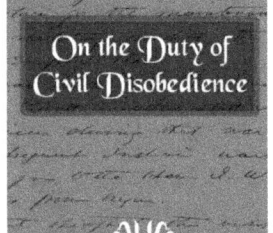

On the Duty of Civil Disobedience
Henry David Thoreau

QTY

Thoreau wrote his famous essay, On the Duty of Civil Disobedience, as a protest against an unjust but popular war and the immoral but popular institution of slave-owning. He did more than write—he declined to pay his taxes, and was hauled off to gaol in consequence. Who can say how much this refusal of his hastened the end of the war and of slavery ?

Law   ISBN: *1-59462-747-9*   **Pages:48**

MSRP $7.45

Dream Psychology Psychoanalysis for Beginners
Sigmund Freud

QTY

Sigmund Freud, born Sigismund Schlomo Freud (May 6, 1856 - September 23, 1939), was a Jewish-Austrian neurologist and psychiatrist who co-founded the psychoanalytic school of psychology. Freud is best known for his theories of the unconscious mind, especially involving the mechanism of repression; his redefinition of sexual desire as mobile and directed towards a wide variety of objects; and his therapeutic techniques, especially his understanding of transference in the therapeutic relationship and the presumed value of dreams as sources of insight into unconscious desires.

Dream Psychology
Psychoanalysis for Beginners

Sigmund Freud

Pages:196

Psychology   ISBN: *1-59462-905-6*   *MSRP $15.45*

The Miracle of Right Thought
Orison Swett Marden

QTY

Believe with all of your heart that you will do what you were made to do. When the mind has once formed the habit of holding cheerful, happy, prosperous pictures, it will not be easy to form the opposite habit. It does not matter how improbable or how far away this realization may see, or how dark the prospects may be, if we visualize them as best we can, as vividly as possible, hold tenaciously to them and vigorously struggle to attain them, they will gradually become actualized, realized in the life. But a desire, a longing without endeavor, a yearning abandoned or held indifferently will vanish without realization.

Pages:360

Self Help   ISBN: *1-59462-644-8*   *MSRP $25.45*

QTY

The Rosicrucian Cosmo-Conception Mystic Christianity by *Max Heindel* — ISBN: *1-59462-188-8* **$38.95**
The Rosicrucian Cosmo-conception is not dogmatic, neither does it appeal to any other authority than the reason of the student. It is: not controversial, but is: sent forth in the, hope that it may help to clear... — New Age/Religion Pages 646

Abandonment To Divine Providence by *Jean-Pierre de Caussade* — ISBN: *1-59462-228-0* **$25.95**
"The Rev. Jean Pierre de Caussade was one of the most remarkable spiritual writers of the Society of Jesus in France in the 18th Century. His death took place at Toulouse in 1751. His works have gone through many editions and have been republished... — Inspirational/Religion Pages 400

Mental Chemistry by *Charles Haanel* — ISBN: *1-59462-192-6* **$23.95**
Mental Chemistry allows the change of material conditions by combining and appropriately utilizing the power of the mind. Much like applied chemistry creates something new and unique out of careful combinations of chemicals the mastery of mental chemistry... — New Age/Business Pages 354

The Letters of Robert Browning and Elizabeth Barret Barrett 1845-1846 vol II — ISBN: *1-59462-193-4* **$35.95**
by *Robert Browning* and *Elizabeth Barrett* — Biographies Pages 596

Gleanings In Genesis (volume I) by *Arthur W. Pink* — ISBN: *1-59462-130-6* **$27.45**
Appropriately has Genesis been termed "the seed plot of the Bible" for in it we have, in germ form, almost all of the great doctrines which are afterwards fully developed in the books of Scripture which follow... — Religion/Inspirational Pages 420

The Master Key by *L. W. de Laurence* — ISBN: *1-59462-001-6* **$30.95**
In no branch of human knowledge has there been a more lively increase of the spirit of research during the past few years than in the study of Psychology, Concentration and Mental Discipline. The requests for authentic lessons in Thought Control, Mental Discipline and... — New Age/Business Pages 422

The Lesser Key Of Solomon Goetia by *L. W. de Laurence* — ISBN: *1-59462-092-X* **$9.95**
This translation of the first book of the "Lernegton" which is now for the first time made accessible to students of Talismanic Magic was done, after careful collation and edition, from numerous Ancient Manuscripts in Hebrew, Latin, and French... — New Age/Occult Pages 92

Rubaiyat Of Omar Khayyam by *Edward Fitzgerald* — ISBN: *1-59462-332-5* **$13.95**
Edward Fitzgerald, whom the world has already learned, in spite of his own efforts to remain within the shadow of anonymity, to look upon as one of the rarest poets of the century, was born at Bredfield, in Suffolk, on the 31st of March, 1809. He was the third son of John Purcell... — Music Pages 172

Ancient Law by *Henry Maine* — ISBN: *1-59462-128-4* **$29.95**
The chief object of the following pages is to indicate some of the earliest ideas of mankind, as they are reflected in Ancient Law, and to point out the relation of those ideas to modern thought. — Religiom/History Pages 452

Far-Away Stories by *William J. Locke* — ISBN: *1-59462-129-2* **$19.45**
"Good wine needs no bush, but a collection of mixed vintages does. And this book is just such a collection. Some of the stories I do not want to remain buried for ever in the museum files of dead magazine-numbers an author's not unpardonable vanity..." — Fiction Pages 272

Life of David Crockett by *David Crockett* — ISBN: *1-59462-250-7* **$27.45**
"Colonel David Crockett was one of the most remarkable men of the times in which he lived. Born in humble life, but gifted with a strong will, an indomitable courage, and unremitting perseverance... — Biographies/New Age Pages 424

Lip-Reading by *Edward Nitchie* — ISBN: *1-59462-206-X* **$25.95**
Edward B. Nitchie, founder of the New York School for the Hard of Hearing, now the Nitchie School of Lip-Reading, Inc, wrote "LIP-READING Principles and Practice". The development and perfecting of this meritorious work on lip-reading was an undertaking... — How-to Pages 400

A Handbook of Suggestive Therapeutics, Applied Hypnotism, Psychic Science — ISBN: *1-59462-214-0* **$24.95**
by *Henry Munro* — Health/New Age/Health/Self-help Pages 376

A Doll's House: and Two Other Plays by *Henrik Ibsen* — ISBN: *1-59462-112-8* **$19.95**
Henrik Ibsen created this classic when in revolutionary 1848 Rome. Introducing some striking concepts in playwriting for the realist genre, this play has been studied the world over. — Fiction/Classics/Plays 308

The Light of Asia by *sir Edwin Arnold* — ISBN: *1-59462-204-3* **$13.95**
In this poetic masterpiece, Edwin Arnold describes the life and teachings of Buddha. The man who was to become known as Buddha to the world was born as Prince Gautama of India but he rejected the worldly riches and abandoned the reigns of power when... — Religion/History/Biographies Pages 170

The Complete Works of Guy de Maupassant by *Guy de Maupassant* — ISBN: *1-59462-157-8* **$16.95**
"For days and days, nights and nights, I had dreamed of that first kiss which was to consecrate our engagement, and I knew not on what spot I should put my lips..." — Fiction/Classics Pages 240

The Art of Cross-Examination by *Francis L. Wellman* — ISBN: *1-59462-309-0* **$26.95**
Written by a renowned trial lawyer, Wellman imparts his experience and uses case studies to explain how to use psychology to extract desired information through questioning. — How-to/Science/Reference Pages 408

Answered or Unanswered? by *Louisa Vaughan* — ISBN: *1-59462-248-5* **$10.95**
Miracles of Faith in China — Religion Pages 112

The Edinburgh Lectures on Mental Science (1909) by *Thomas* — ISBN: *1-59462-008-3* **$11.95**
This book contains the substance of a course of lectures recently given by the writer in the Queen Street Hail, Edinburgh. Its purpose is to indicate the Natural Principles governing the relation between Mental Action and Material Conditions... — New Age/Psychology Pages 148

Ayesha by *H. Rider Haggard* — ISBN: *1-59462-301-5* **$24.95**
Verily and indeed it is the unexpected that happens! Probably if there was one person upon the earth from whom the Editor of this, and of a certain previous history, did not expect to hear again... — Classics Pages 380

Ayala's Angel by *Anthony Trollope* — ISBN: *1-59462-352-X* **$29.95**
The two girls were both pretty, but Lucy who was twenty-one who supposed to be simple and comparatively unattractive, whereas Ayala was credited, as her Bombwhat romantic name might show, with poetic charm and a taste for romance. Ayala when her father died was nineteen... — Fiction Pages 484

The American Commonwealth by *James Bryce* — ISBN: *1-59462-286-8* **$34.45**
An interpretation of American democratic political theory. It examines political mechanics and society from the perspective of Scotsman James Bryce — Politics Pages 572

Stories of the Pilgrims by *Margaret P. Pumphrey* — ISBN: *1-59462-116-0* **$17.95**
This book explores pilgrims religious oppression in England as well as their escape to Holland and eventual crossing to America on the Mayflower, and their early days in New England... — History Pages 268

QTY

The Fasting Cure *by Sinclair Upton*   ISBN: *1-59462-222-1* **$13.95**
In the Cosmopolitan Magazine for May, 1910, and in the Contemporary Review (London) for April, 1910, I published an article dealing with my experiences in fasting. I have written a great many magazine articles, but never one which attracted so much attention... New Age/Self Help/Health Pages 164

Hebrew Astrology *by Sepharial*   ISBN: *1-59462-308-2* **$13.45**
In these days of advanced thinking it is a matter of common observation that we have left many of the old landmarks behind and that we are now pressing forward to greater heights and to a wider horizon than that which represented the mind-content of our progenitors... Astrology Pages 144

Thought Vibration or The Law of Attraction in the Thought World   ISBN: *1-59462-127-6* **$12.95**
by William Walker Atkinson   *Psychology/Religion Pages 144*

Optimism *by Helen Keller*   ISBN: *1-59462-108-X* **$15.95**
Helen Keller was blind, deaf, and mute since 19 months old, yet famously learned how to overcome these handicaps, communicate with the world, and spread her lectures promoting optimism. An inspiring read for everyone... Biographies/Inspirational Pages 84

Sara Crewe *by Frances Burnett*   ISBN: *1-59462-360-0* **$9.45**
In the first place, Miss Minchin lived in London. Her home was a large, dull, tall one, in a large, dull square, where all the houses were alike, and all the sparrows were alike, and where all the door-knockers made the same heavy sound... Childrens/Classic Pages 88

The Autobiography of Benjamin Franklin *by Benjamin Franklin*   ISBN: *1-59462-135-7* **$24.95**
The Autobiography of Benjamin Franklin has probably been more extensively read than any other American historical work, and no other book of its kind has had such ups and downs of fortune. Franklin lived for many years in England, where he was agent... Biographies/History Pages 332

Name	
Email	
Telephone	
Address	
City, State ZIP	

☐ **Credit Card**   ☐ **Check / Money Order**

Credit Card Number	
Expiration Date	
Signature	

Please Mail to: Book Jungle
PO Box 2226
Champaign, IL 61825
or Fax to: 630-214-0564

ORDERING INFORMATION

web: *www.bookjungle.com*
email: *sales@bookjungle.com*
fax: *630-214-0564*
mail: *Book Jungle PO Box 2226 Champaign, IL 61825*
or PayPal *to sales@bookjungle.com*

Please contact us for bulk discounts

DIRECT-ORDER TERMS

**20% Discount if You Order
Two or More Books**
Free Domestic Shipping!
Accepted: Master Card, Visa,
Discover, American Express

www.ingramcontent.com/pod-product-compliance
Lightning Source LLC
Chambersburg PA
CBHW080747250626
47162CB00010B/3048